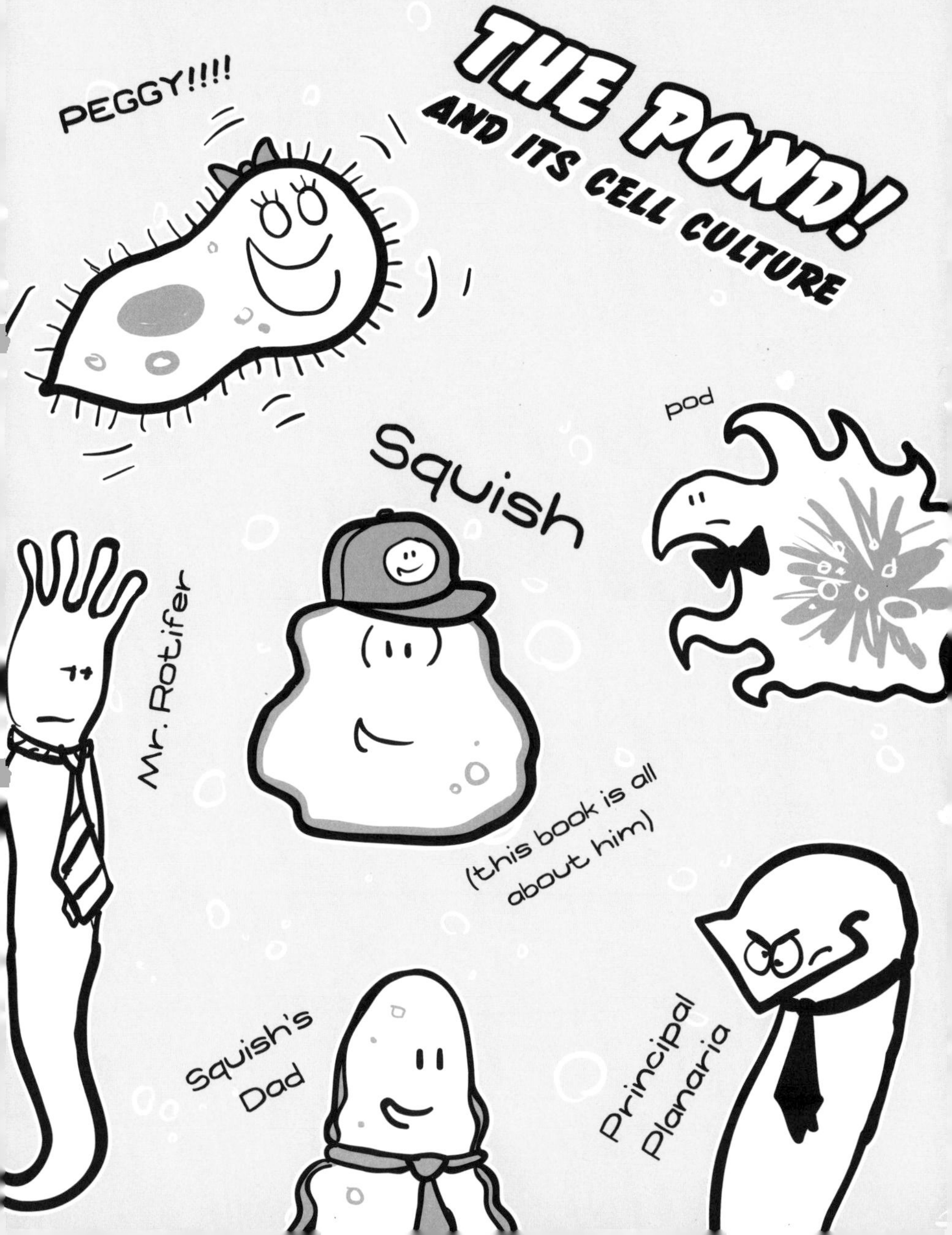
THE POND!
AND ITS CELL CULTURE
PEGGY!!!!
pod
Squish
Mr. Rotifer
(this book is all about him)
Squish's Dad
Principal Planaria

Read ALL the SQUISH books!

#1 SQUISH: Super Amoeba
#2 SQUISH: Brave New Pond
#3 SQUISH: The Power of the Parasite
#4 SQUISH: Captain Disaster
#5 SQUISH: Game On!
#6 SQUISH: Fear the Amoeba
#7 SQUISH: Deadly Disease of Doom
#8 SQUISH: Pod vs. Pod

squish
POD VS. POD

BY JENNIFER L. HOLM & MATTHEW HOLM

RANDOM HOUSE 🏠 NEW YORK

This is a work of fiction. Names, characters, places, and incidents either are the product of the authors' imagination or are used fictitiously. Any resemblance to actual persons, living or dead, events, or locales is entirely coincidental.

Published in the United States by Random House Children's Books, a division of Penguin Random House LLC, New York.

Random House and the colophon are registered trademarks of Penguin Random House LLC.

Visit us on the Web! randomhousekids.com

Educators and librarians, for a variety of teaching tools, visit us at RHTeachersLibrarians.com

Library of Congress Cataloging-in-Publication Data is available upon request.

ISBN 978-0-307-98308-4 (trade) —
ISBN 978-0-307-98309-1 (lib. bdg.) —
ISBN 978-0-307-98310-7 (ebook)

MANUFACTURED IN MALAYSIA 10 9 8 7 6 5 4 3 2
First Edition

Random House Children's Books supports the First Amendment and celebrates the right to read.

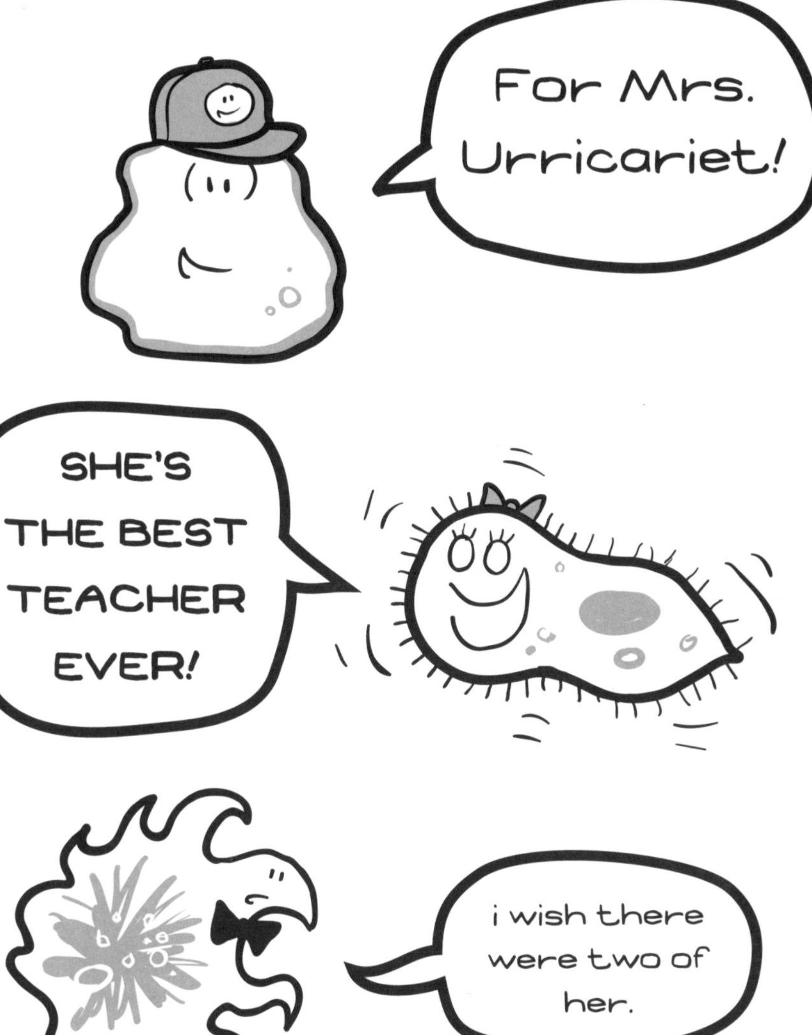
For Mrs. Urricariet!
SHE'S THE BEST TEACHER EVER!
i wish there were two of her.

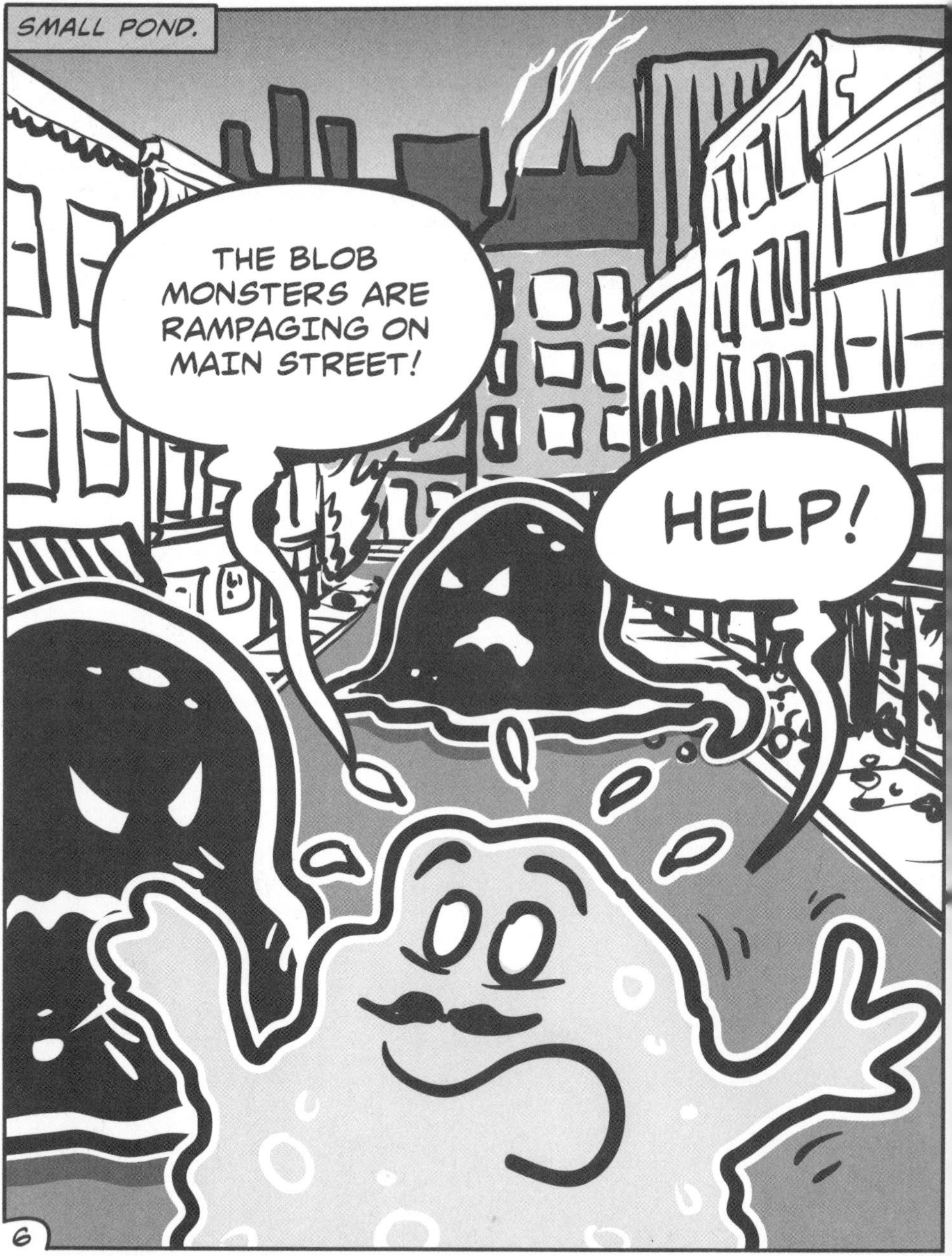
SMALL POND.
THE BLOB MONSTERS ARE RAMPAGING ON MAIN STREET!
HELP!

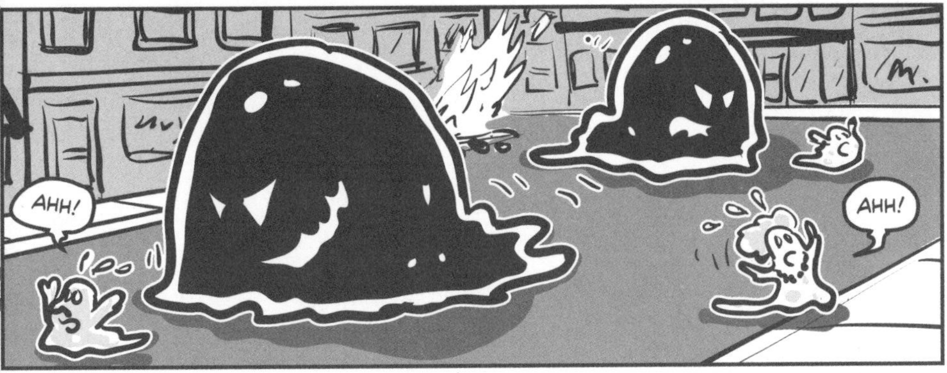
AHH!
AHH!

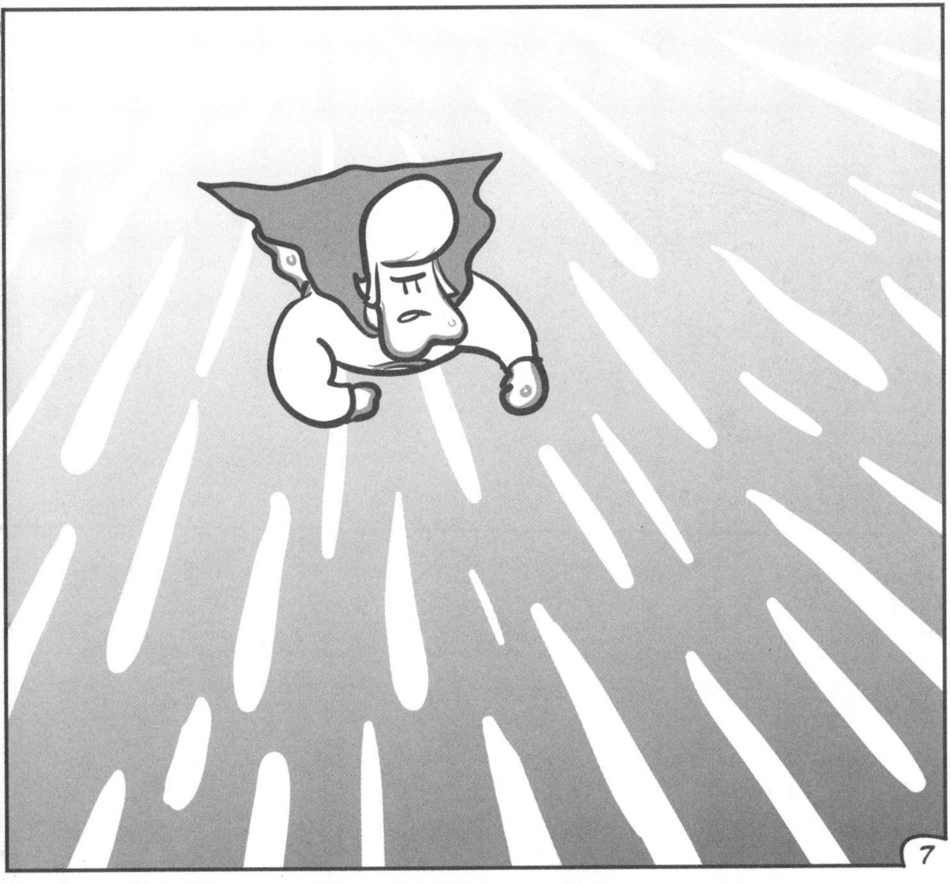

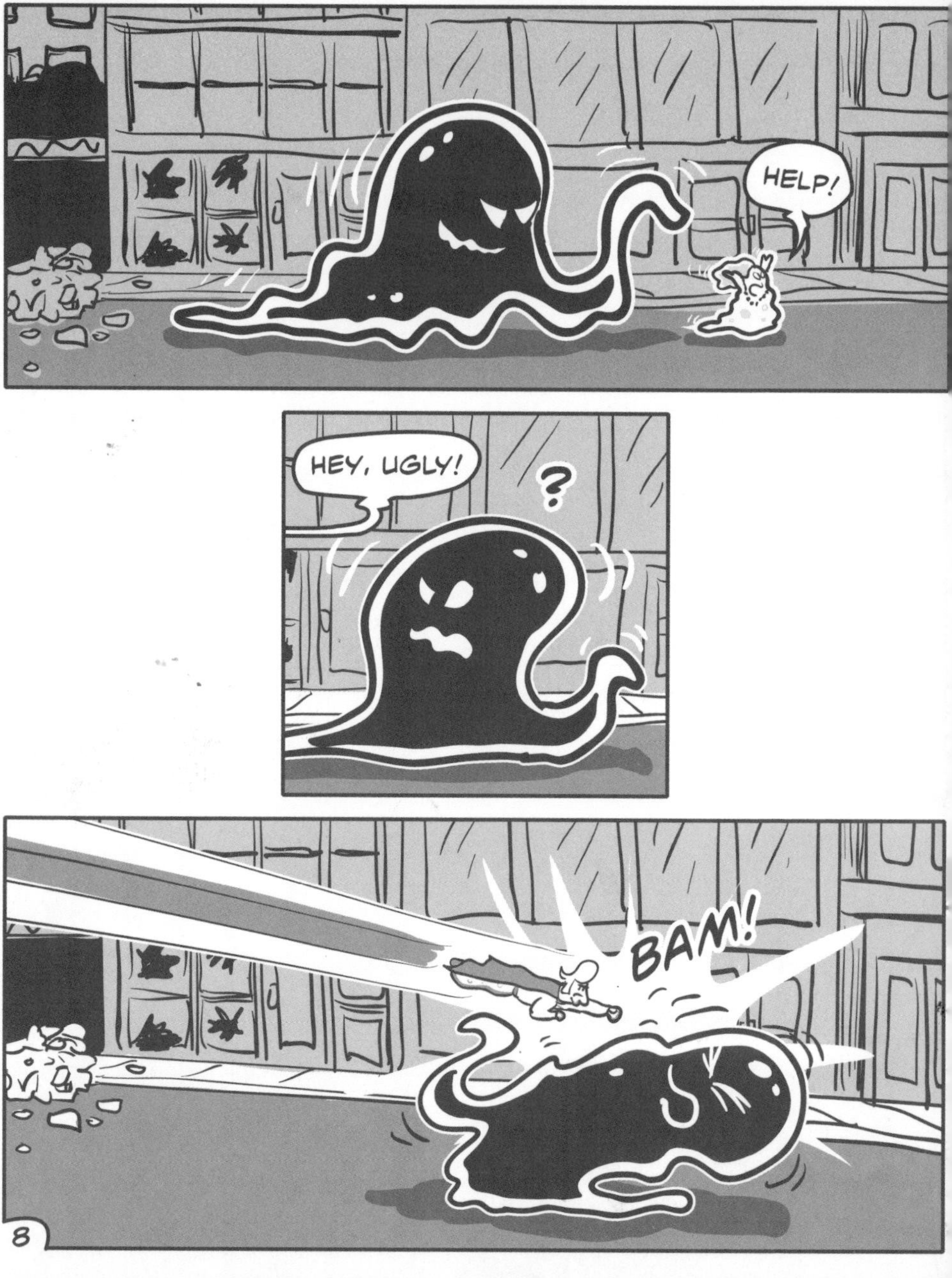
HELP!
HEY, UGLY!
?
BAM!

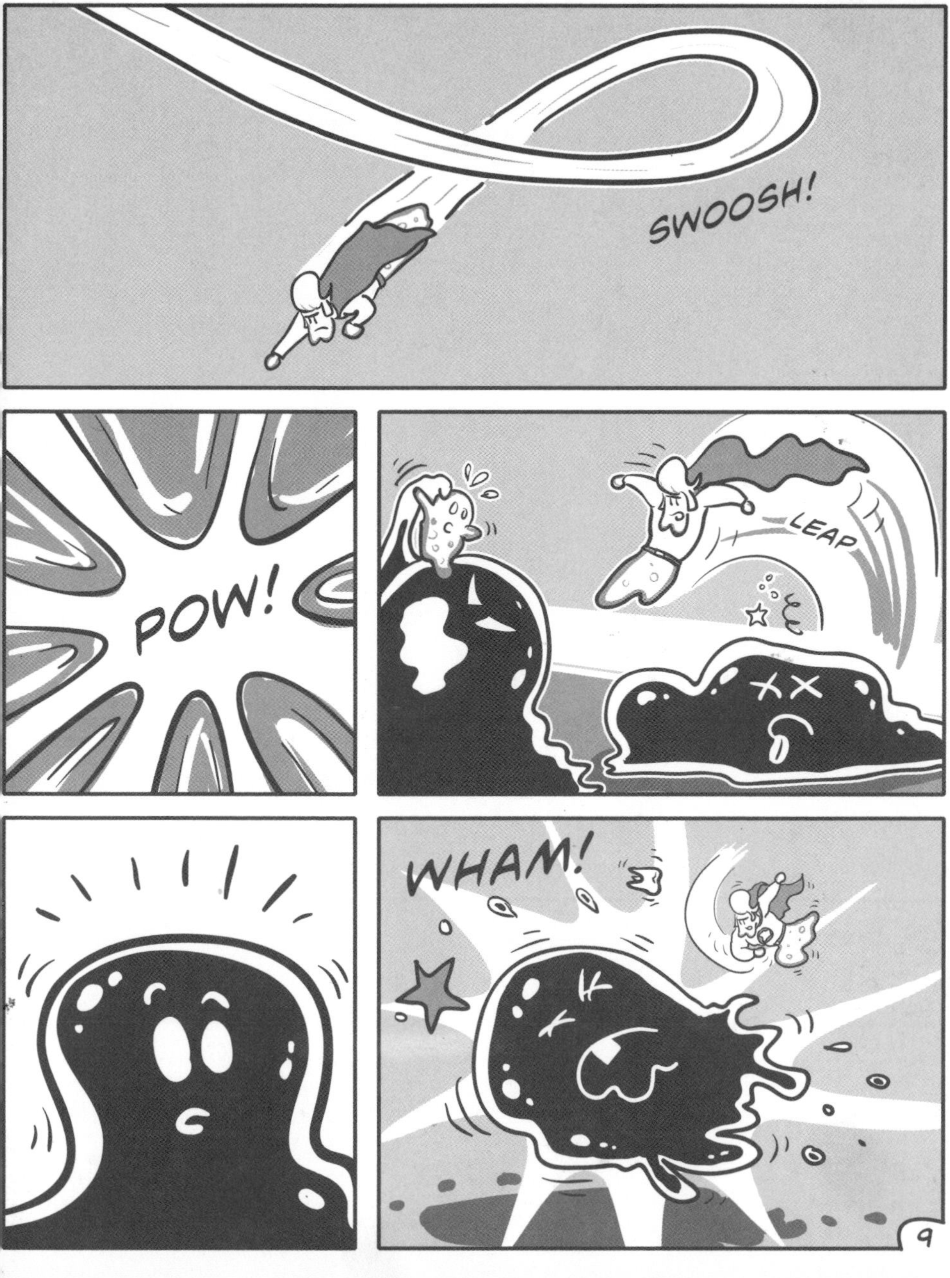
SWOOSH!
POW!
LEAP
WHAM!

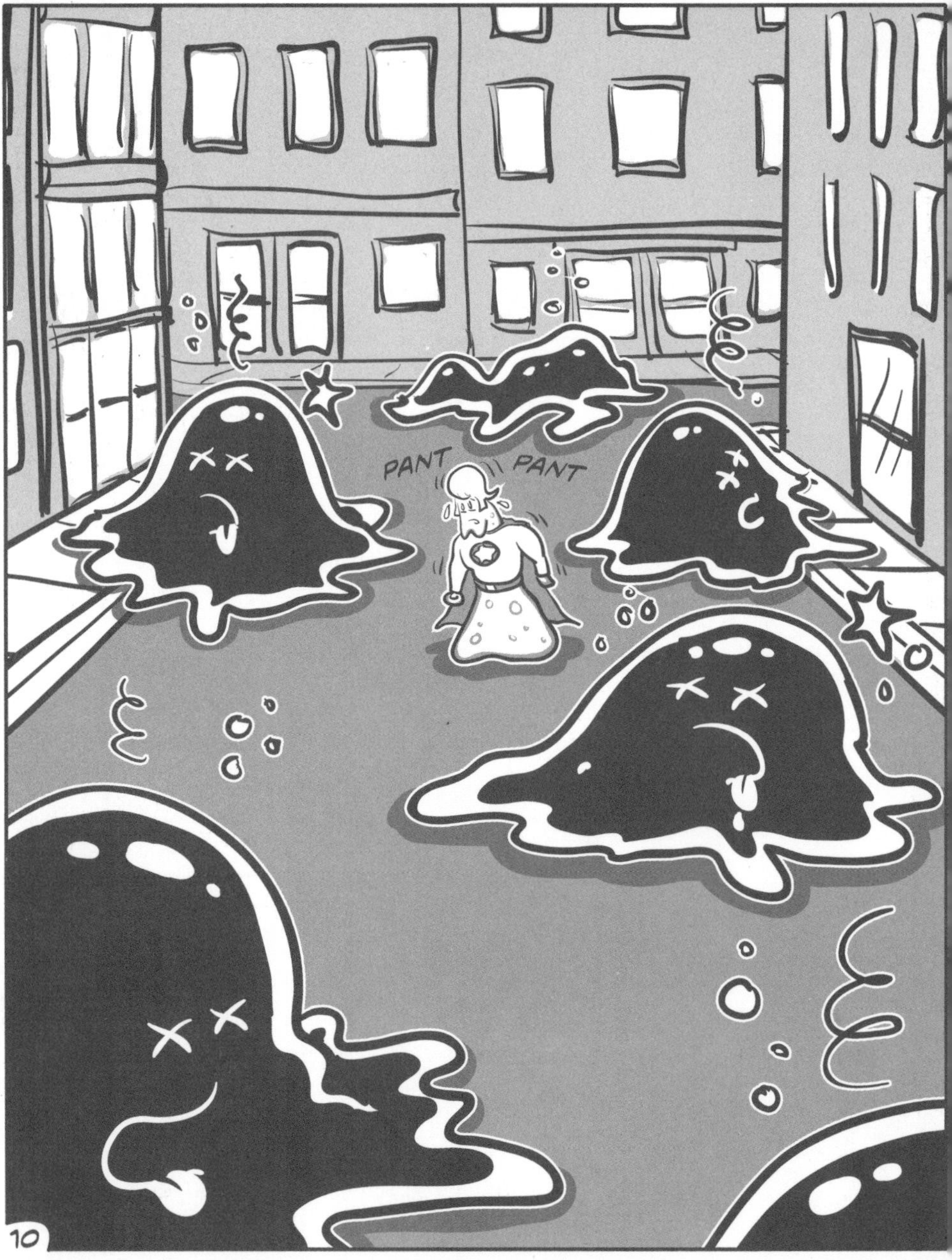
PANT
PANT

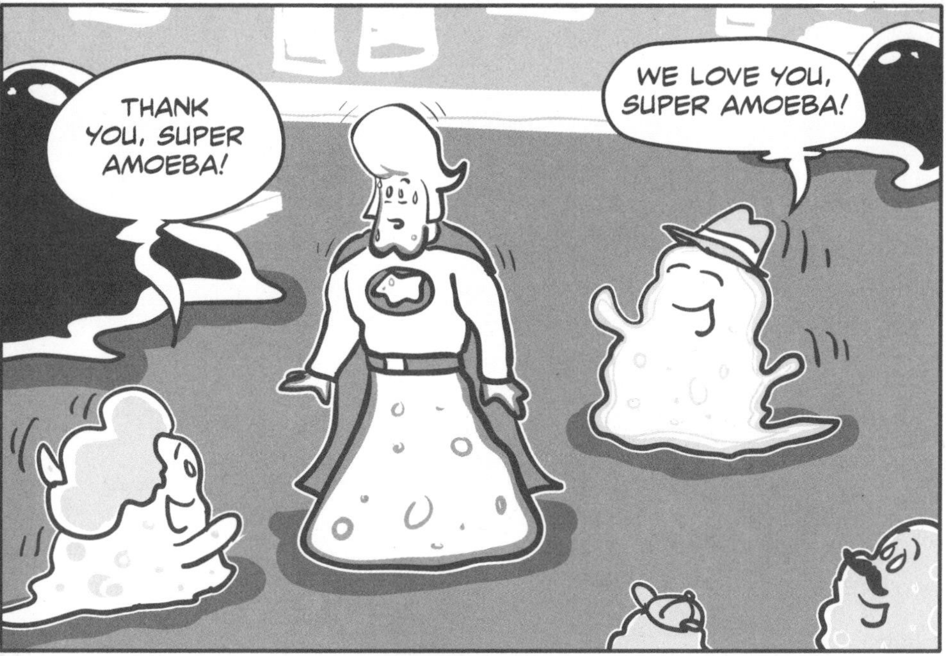
THANK YOU, SUPER AMOEBA!
WE LOVE YOU, SUPER AMOEBA!

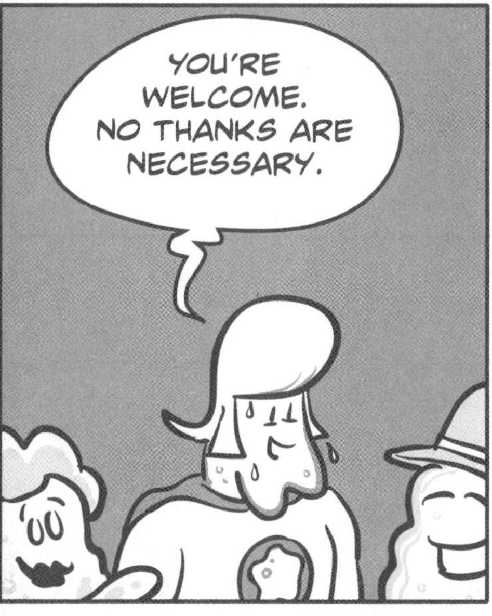
YOU'RE WELCOME. NO THANKS ARE NECESSARY.

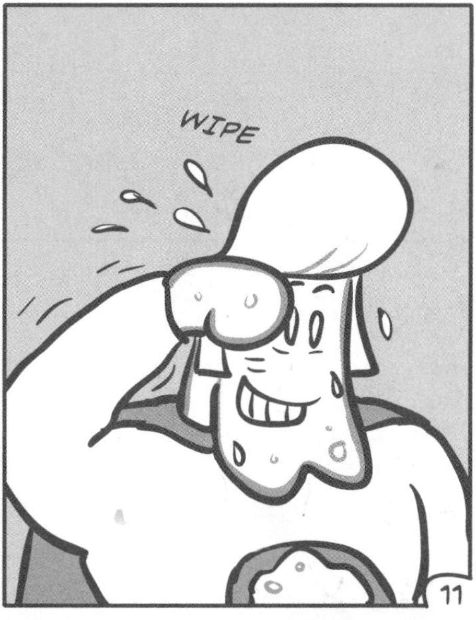
WIPE

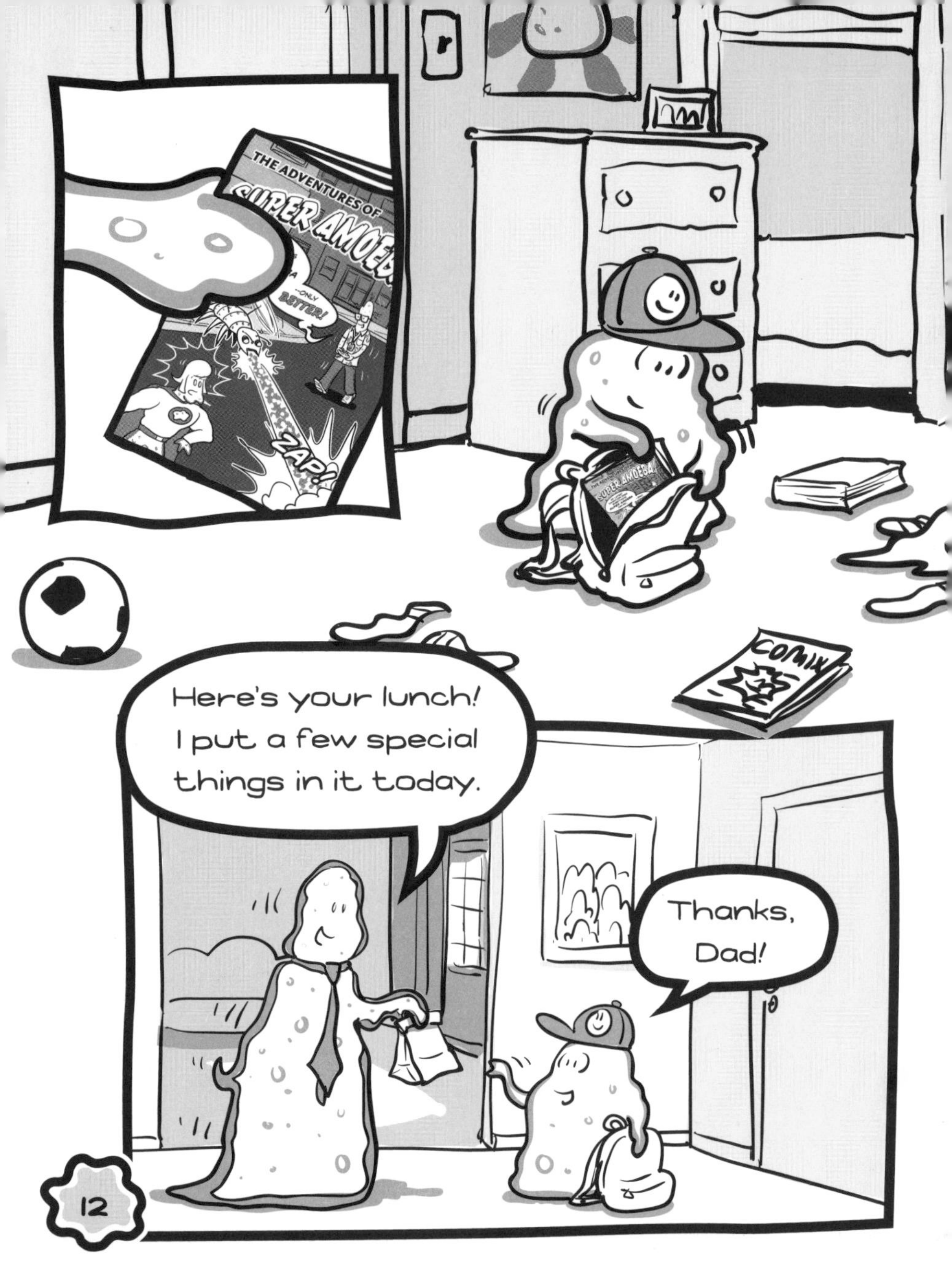
THE ADVENTURES OF
SUPER AMOEBA
--ONLY BETTER!
ZAP!
COMIX
Here's your lunch! I put a few special things in it today.
Thanks, Dad!

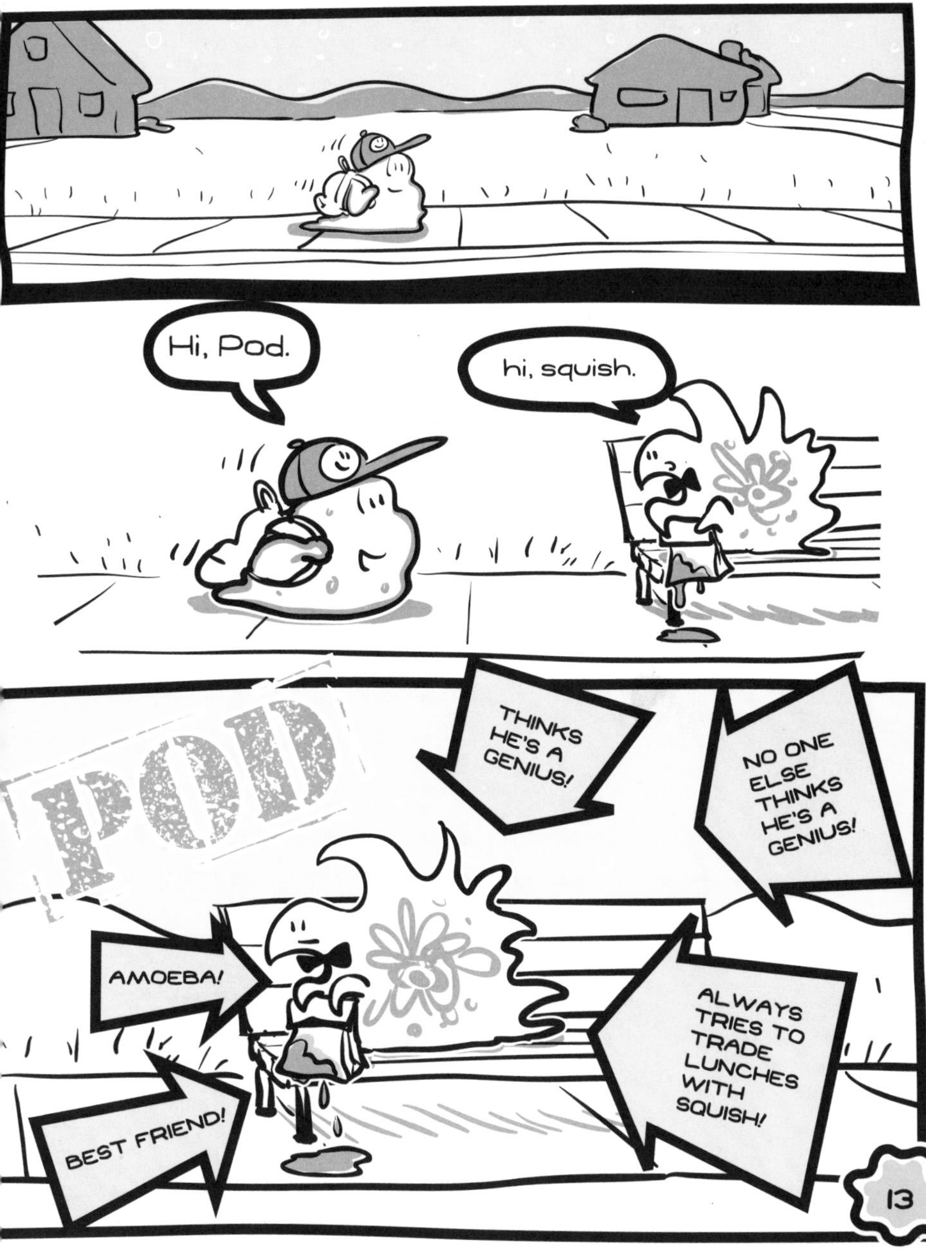
Hi, Pod.
hi, squish.
POD
THINKS HE'S A GENIUS!
NO ONE ELSE THINKS HE'S A GENIUS!
AMOEBA!
ALWAYS TRIES TO TRADE LUNCHES WITH SQUISH!
BEST FRIEND!

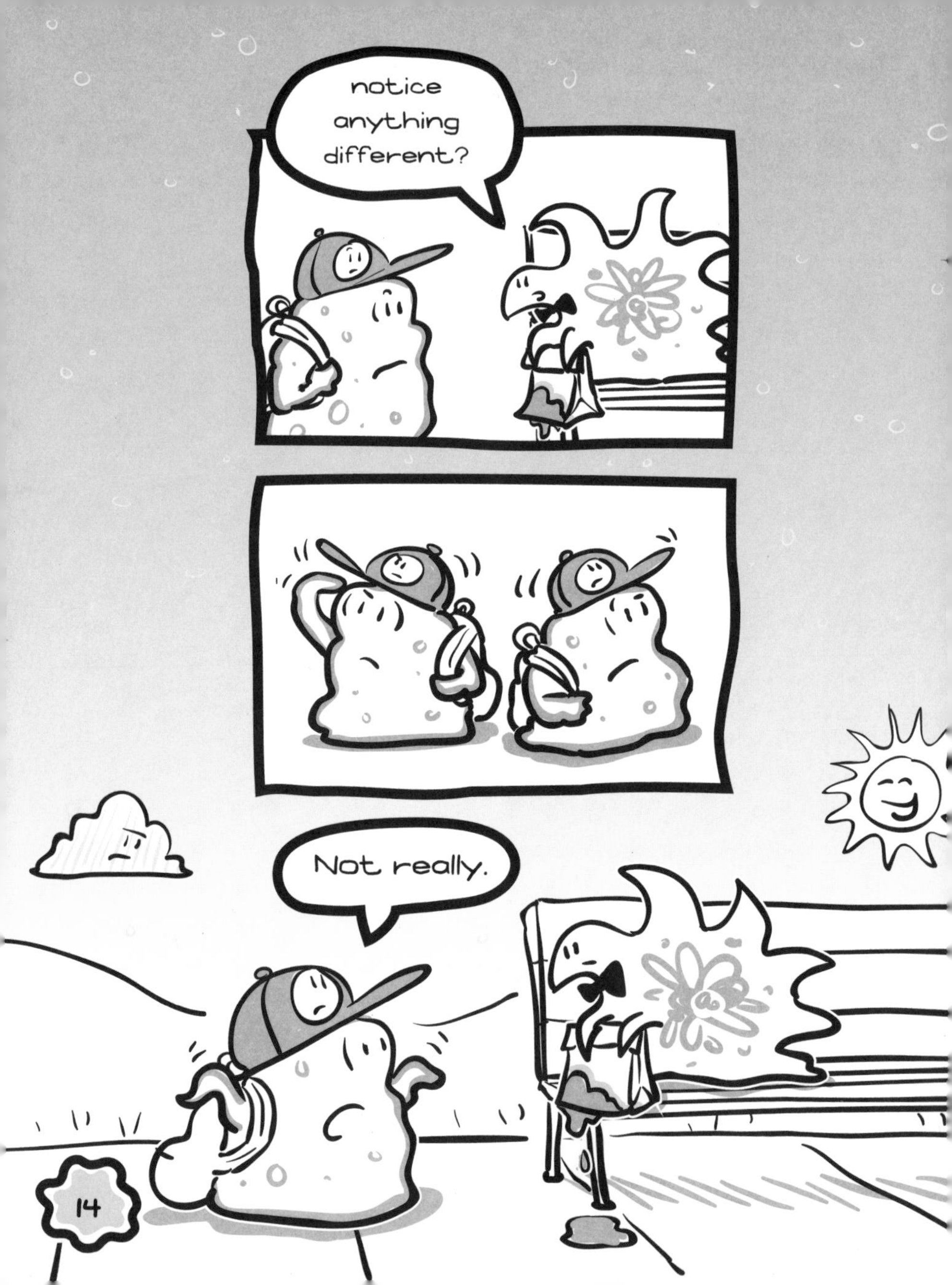
notice anything different?
Not really.

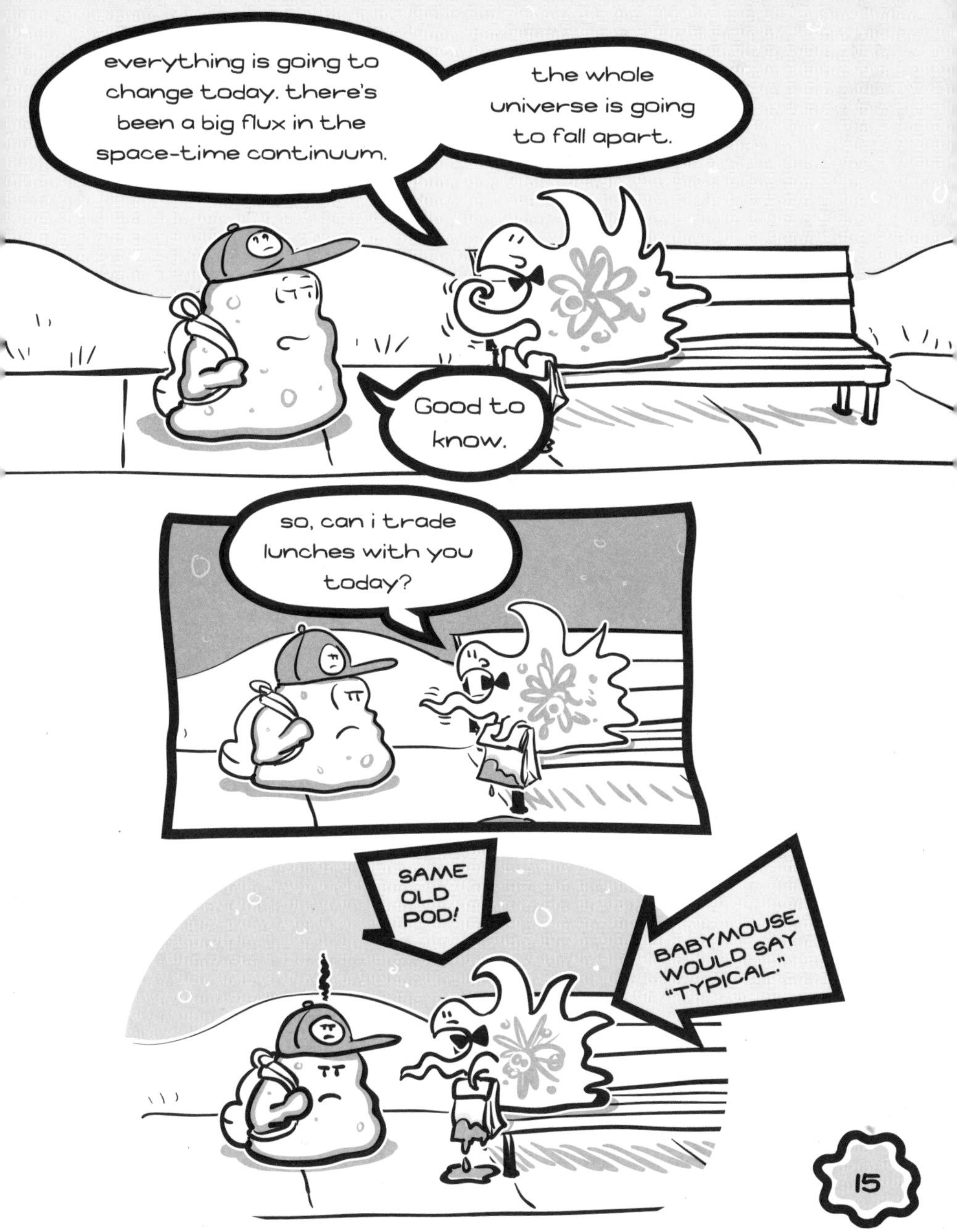

everything is going to change today. there's been a big flux in the space-time continuum.
the whole universe is going to fall apart.
Good to know.
so, can i trade lunches with you today?
SAME OLD POD!
BABYMOUSE WOULD SAY "TYPICAL."

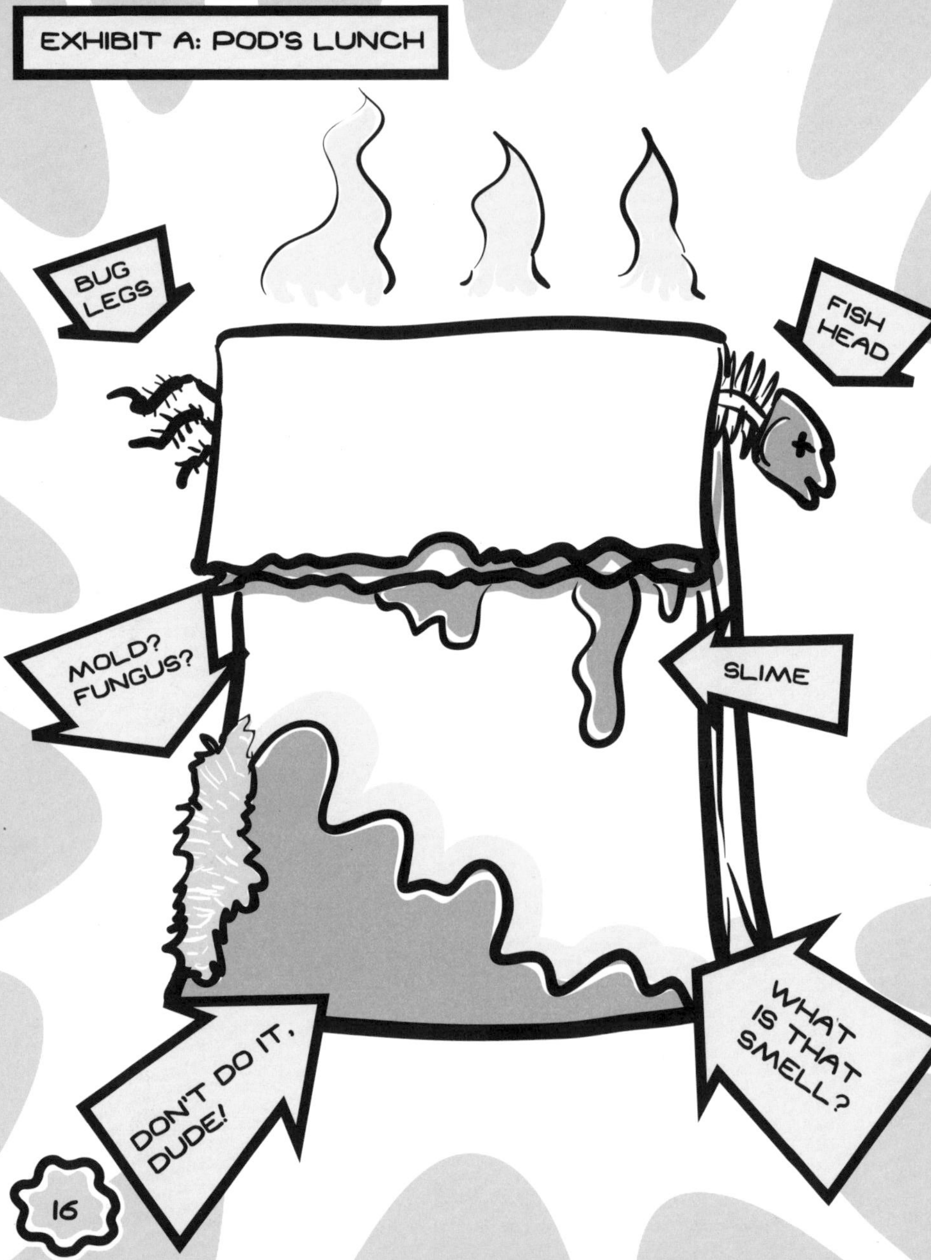
EXHIBIT A: POD'S LUNCH
BUG LEGS
FISH HEAD
MOLD? FUNGUS?
SLIME
DON'T DO IT, DUDE!
WHAT IS THAT SMELL?

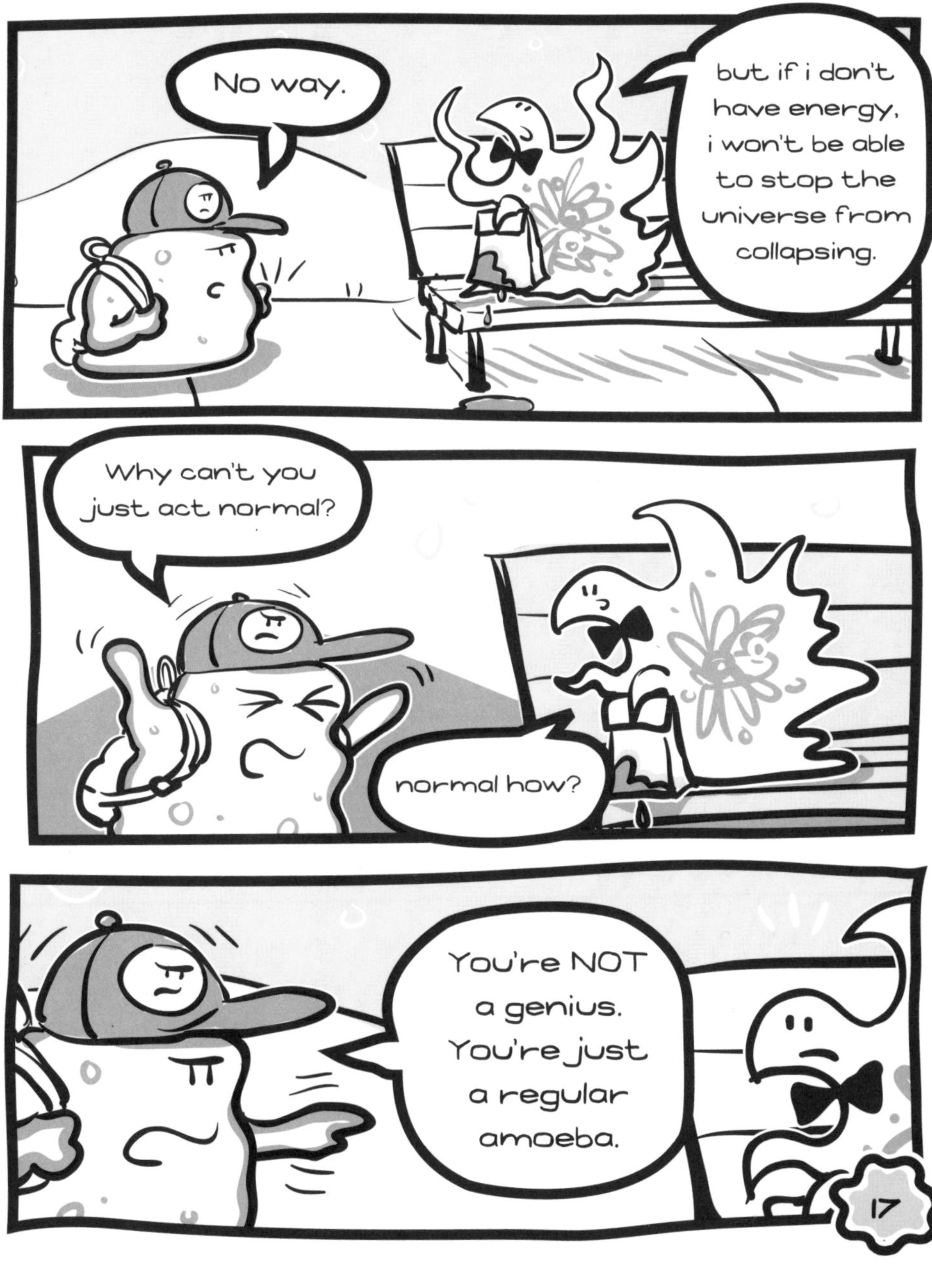
No way.
but if i don't have energy, i won't be able to stop the universe from collapsing.
Why can't you just act normal?
normal how?
You're NOT a genius. You're just a regular amoeba.

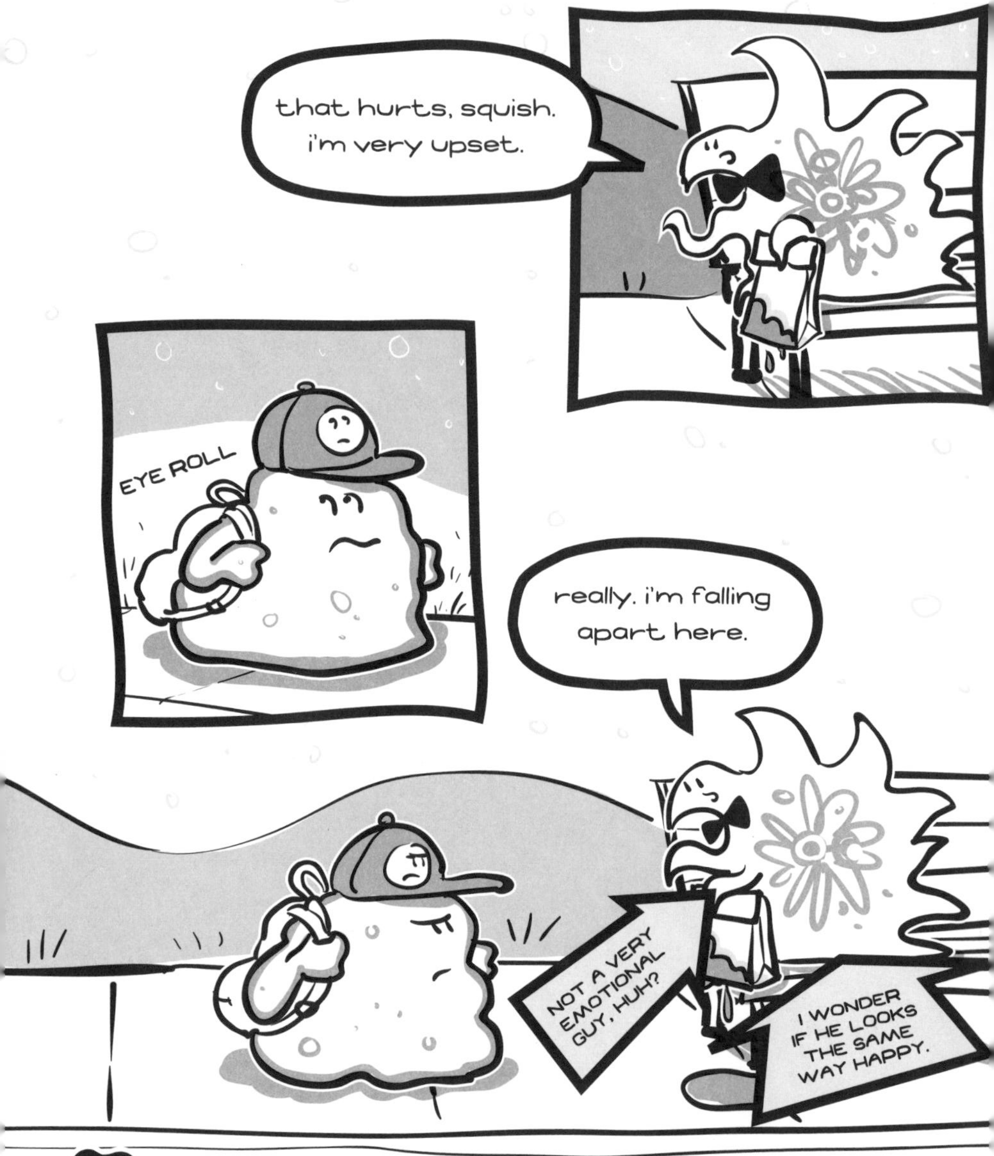
that hurts, squish. i'm very upset.
EYE ROLL
really. i'm falling apart here.
NOT A VERY EMOTIONAL GUY, HUH?
I WONDER IF HE LOOKS THE SAME WAY HAPPY.

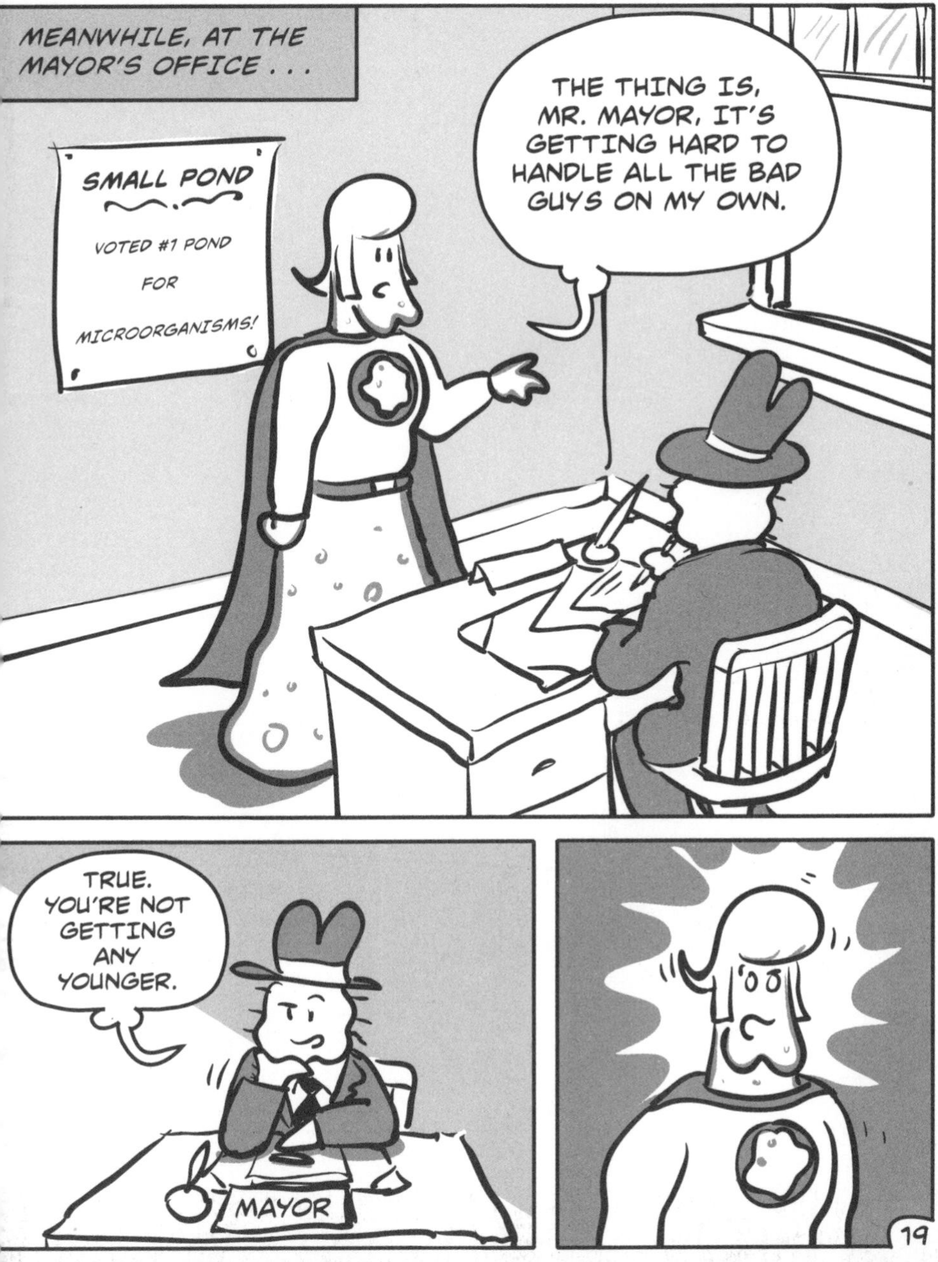
MEANWHILE, AT THE MAYOR'S OFFICE . . .
SMALL POND
VOTED #1 POND FOR MICROORGANISMS!
THE THING IS, MR. MAYOR, IT'S GETTING HARD TO HANDLE ALL THE BAD GUYS ON MY OWN.
TRUE. YOU'RE NOT GETTING ANY YOUNGER.
MAYOR

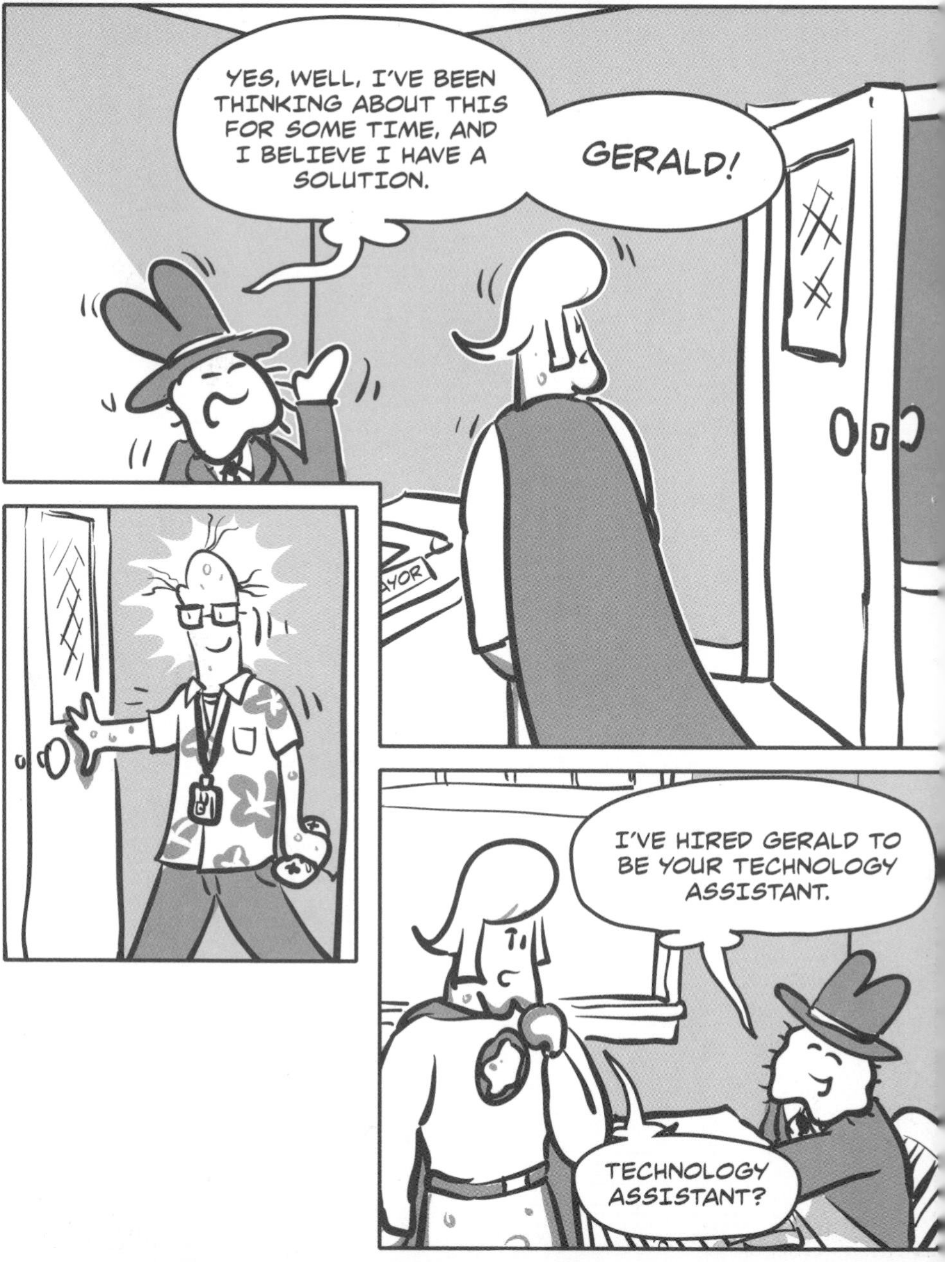

YES, WELL, I'VE BEEN THINKING ABOUT THIS FOR SOME TIME, AND I BELIEVE I HAVE A SOLUTION.
GERALD!
I'VE HIRED GERALD TO BE YOUR TECHNOLOGY ASSISTANT.
TECHNOLOGY ASSISTANT?

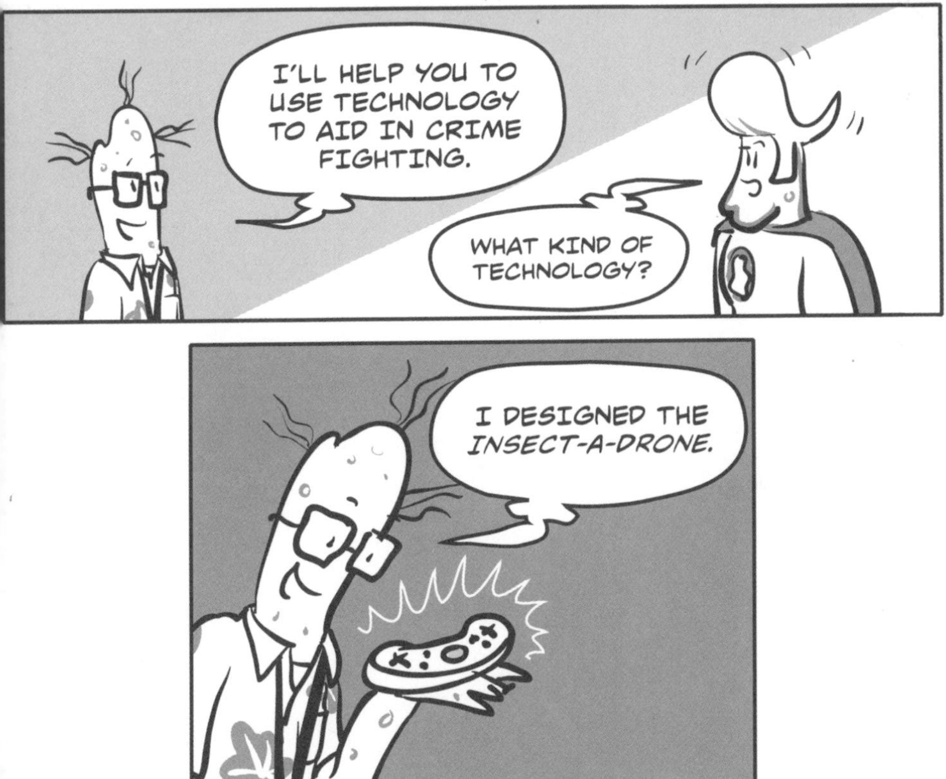
I'LL HELP YOU TO USE TECHNOLOGY TO AID IN CRIME FIGHTING.
WHAT KIND OF TECHNOLOGY?
I DESIGNED THE *INSECT-A-DRONE.*
WHIRRRRR...

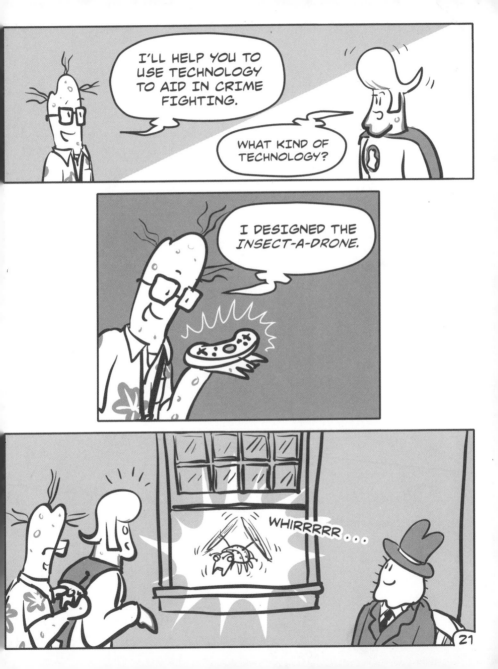

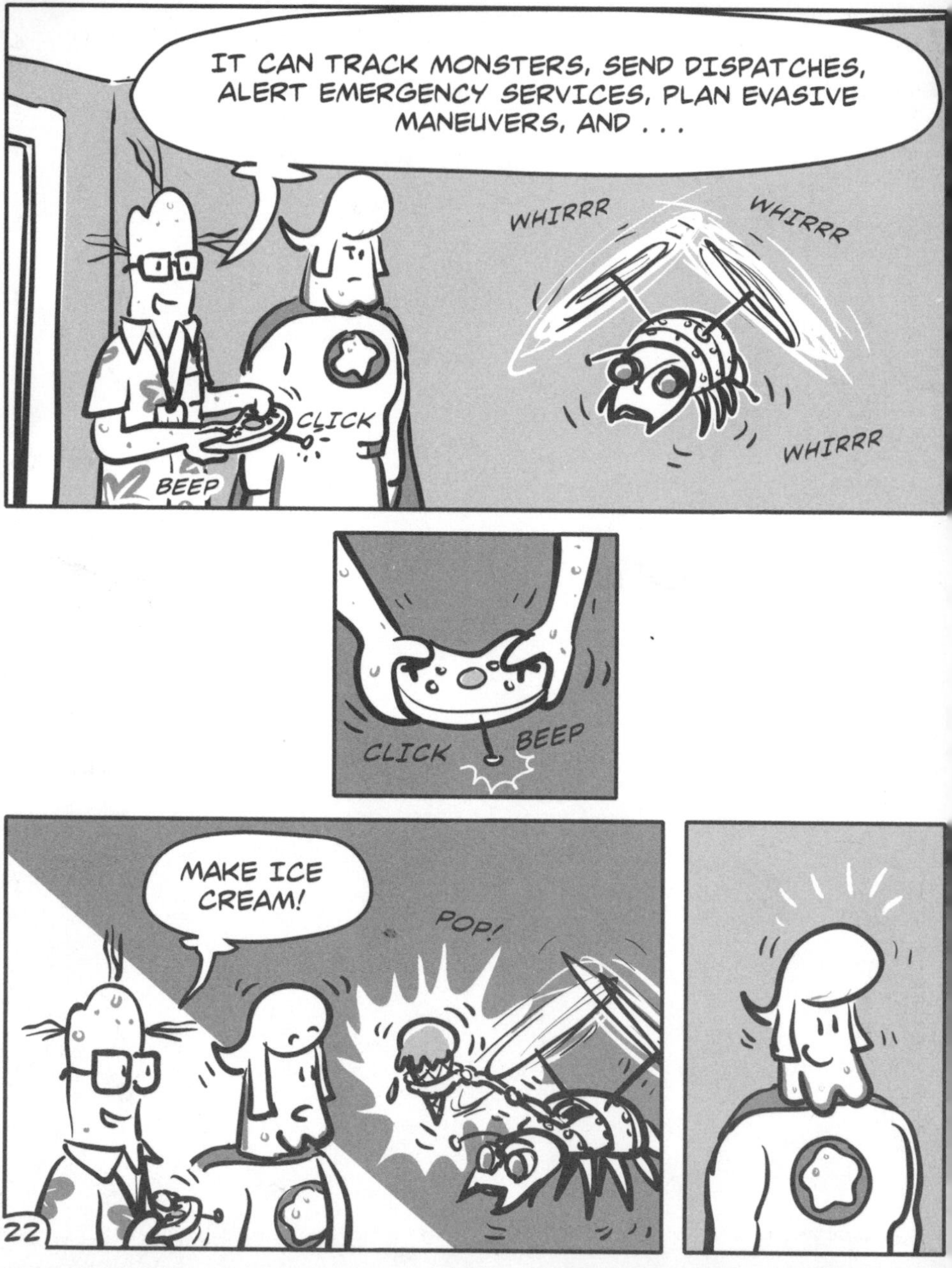
IT CAN TRACK MONSTERS, SEND DISPATCHES, ALERT EMERGENCY SERVICES, PLAN EVASIVE MANEUVERS, AND . . .
WHIRRR
WHIRRR
CLICK
BEEP
WHIRRR
CLICK
BEEP
MAKE ICE CREAM!
POP!

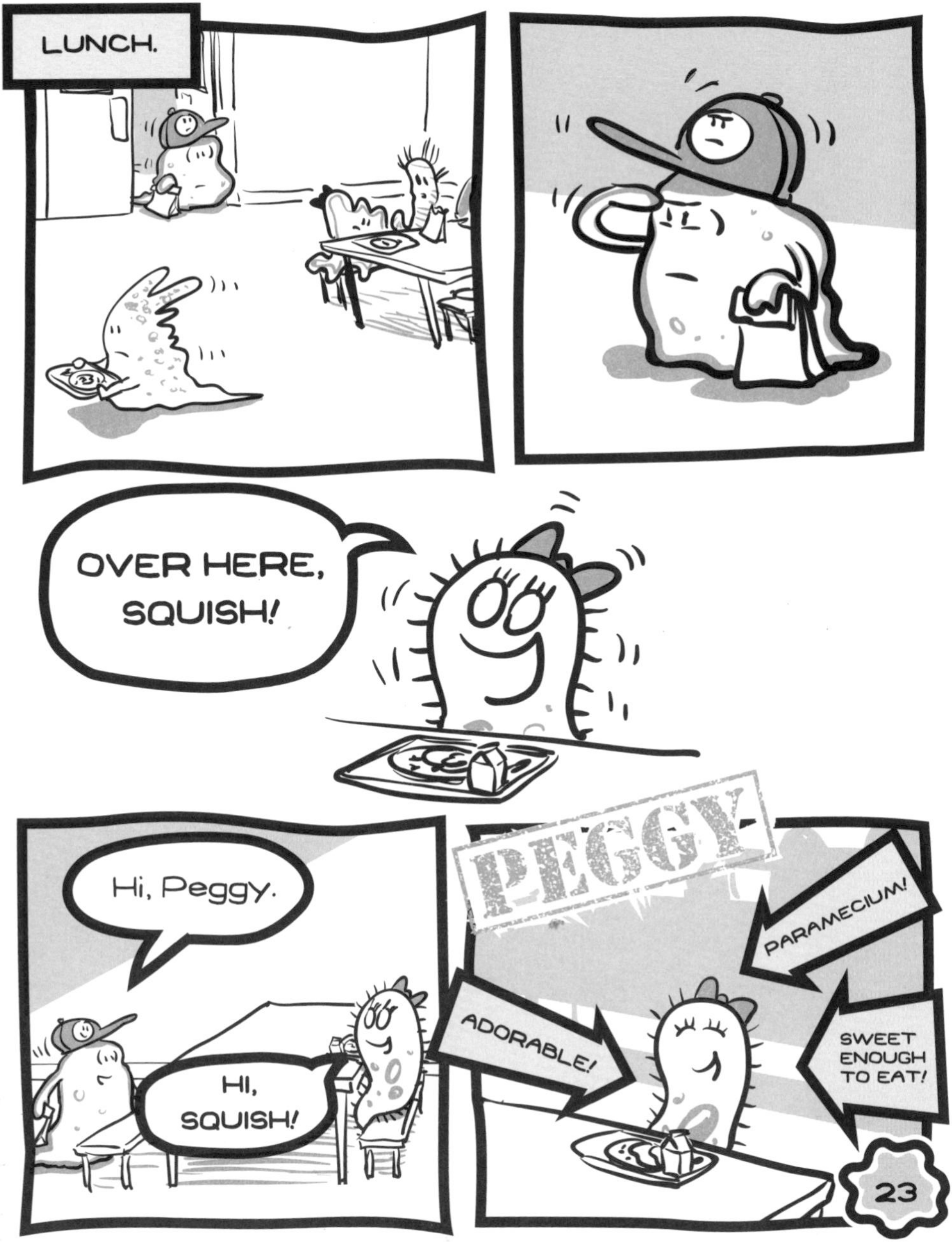
LUNCH.
OVER HERE, SQUISH!
Hi, Peggy.
HI, SQUISH!
PEGGY
PARAMECIUM!
ADORABLE!
SWEET ENOUGH TO EAT!

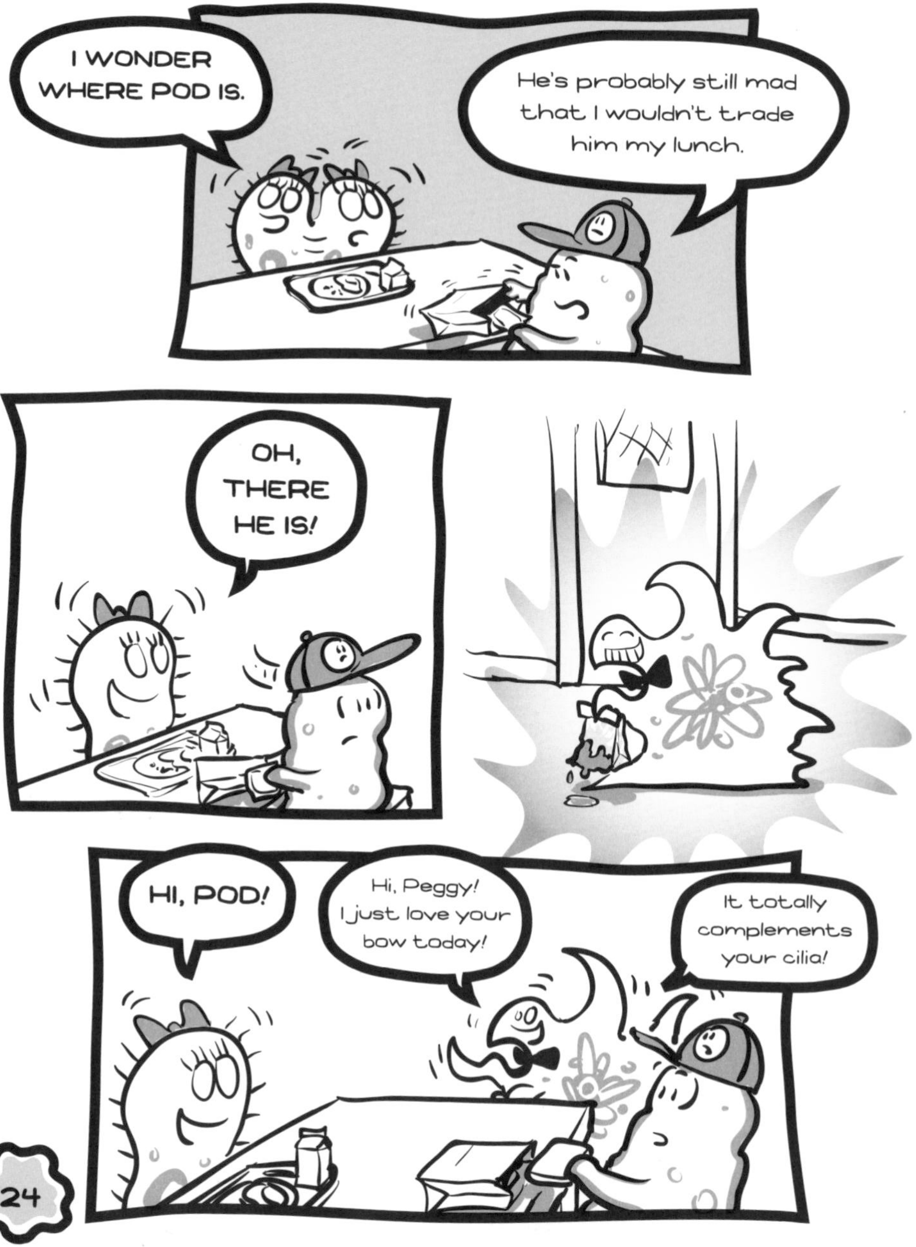
I WONDER WHERE POD IS.
He's probably still mad that I wouldn't trade him my lunch.
OH, THERE HE IS!
HI, POD!
Hi, Peggy! I just love your bow today!
It totally complements your cilia!

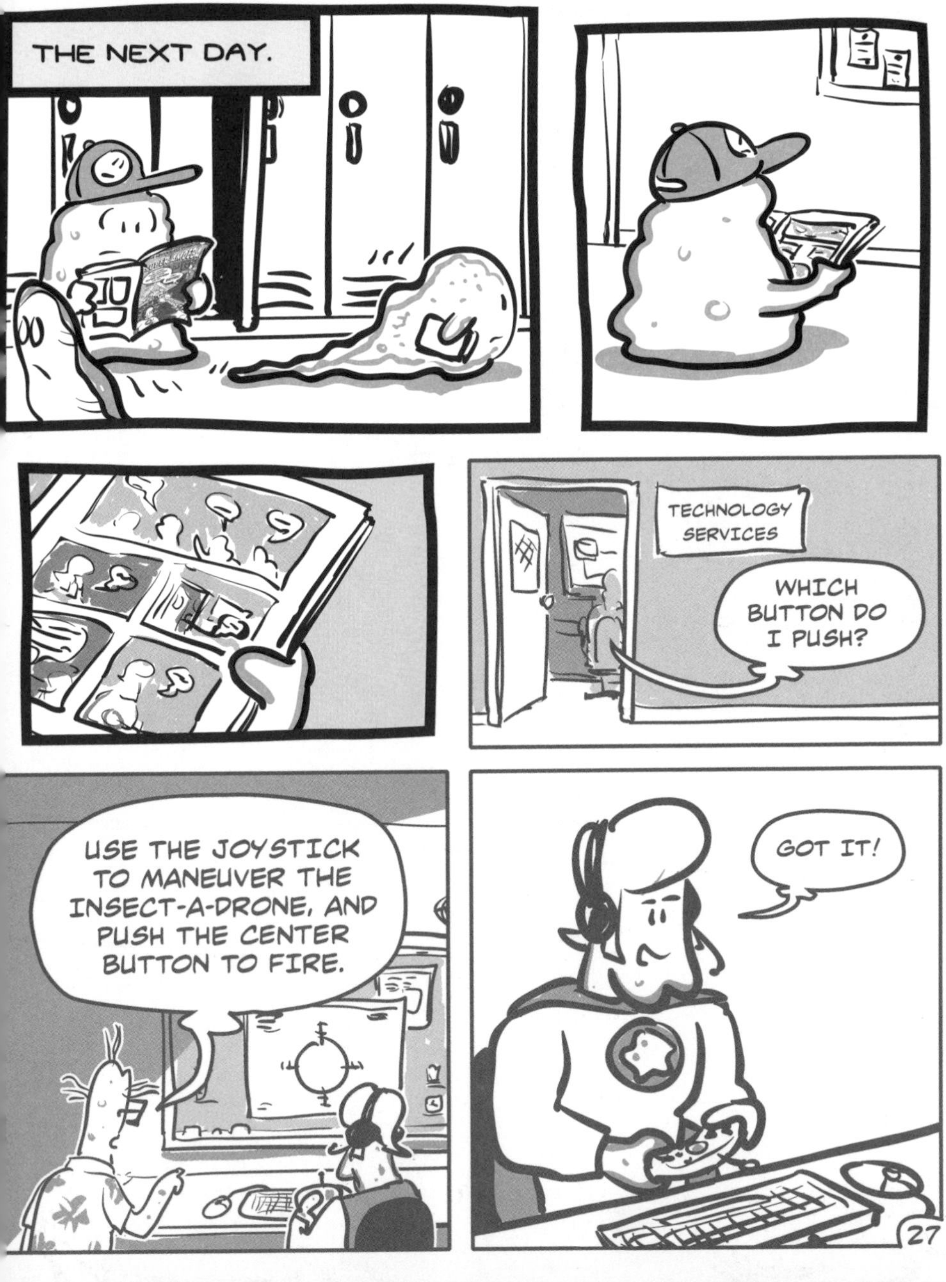
THE NEXT DAY.
TECHNOLOGY SERVICES
WHICH BUTTON DO I PUSH?
USE THE JOYSTICK TO MANEUVER THE INSECT-A-DRONE, AND PUSH THE CENTER BUTTON TO FIRE.
GOT IT!

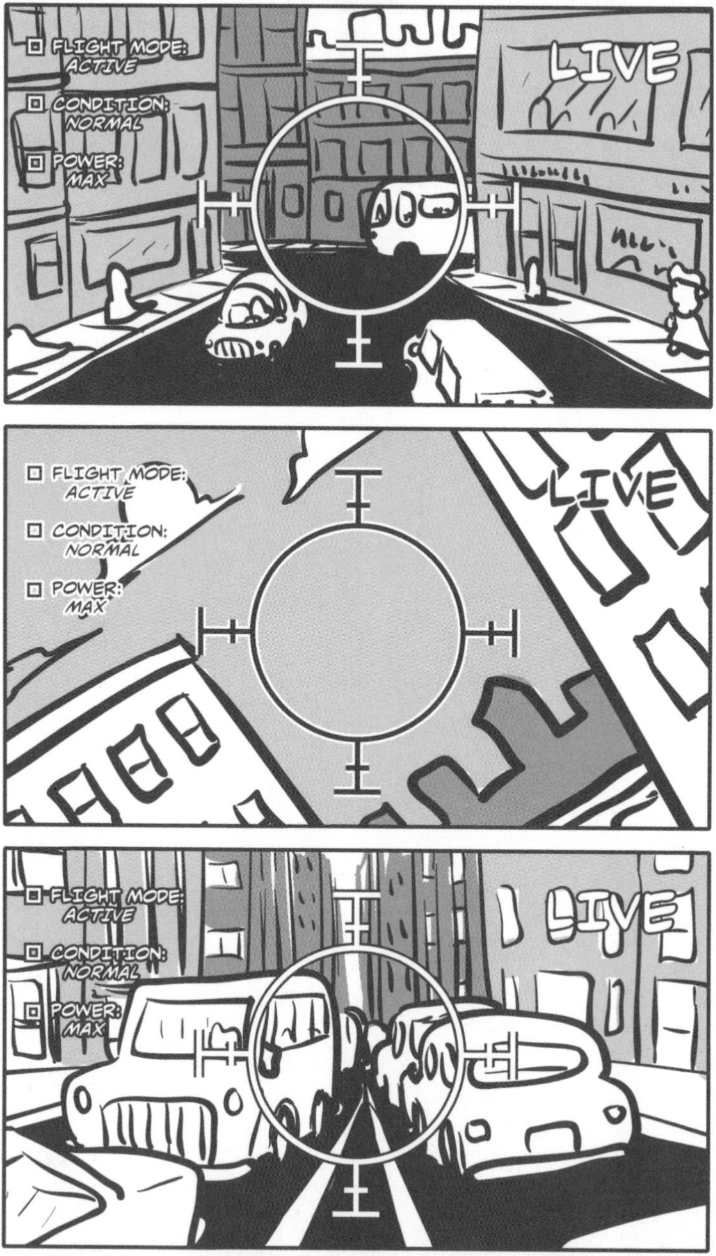
FLIGHT MODE: ACTIVE
CONDITION: NORMAL
POWER: MAX
LIVE
FLIGHT MODE: ACTIVE
CONDITION: NORMAL
POWER: MAX
LIVE
FLIGHT MODE: ACTIVE
CONDITION: NORMAL
POWER: MAX
LIVE

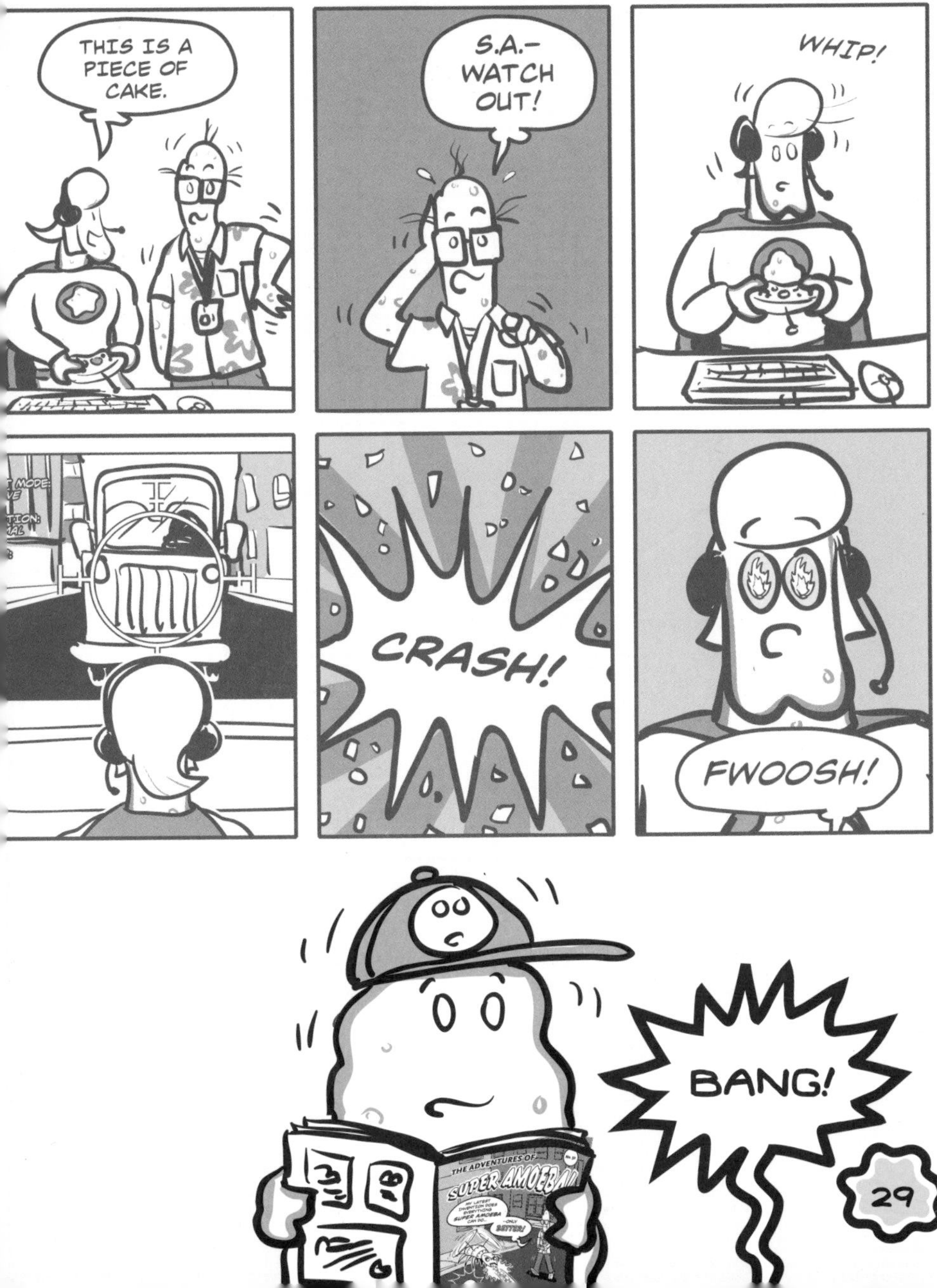
THIS IS A PIECE OF CAKE.
S.A.– WATCH OUT!
WHIP!
CRASH!
FWOOSH!
THE ADVENTURES OF
SUPER AMOEBA
BANG!

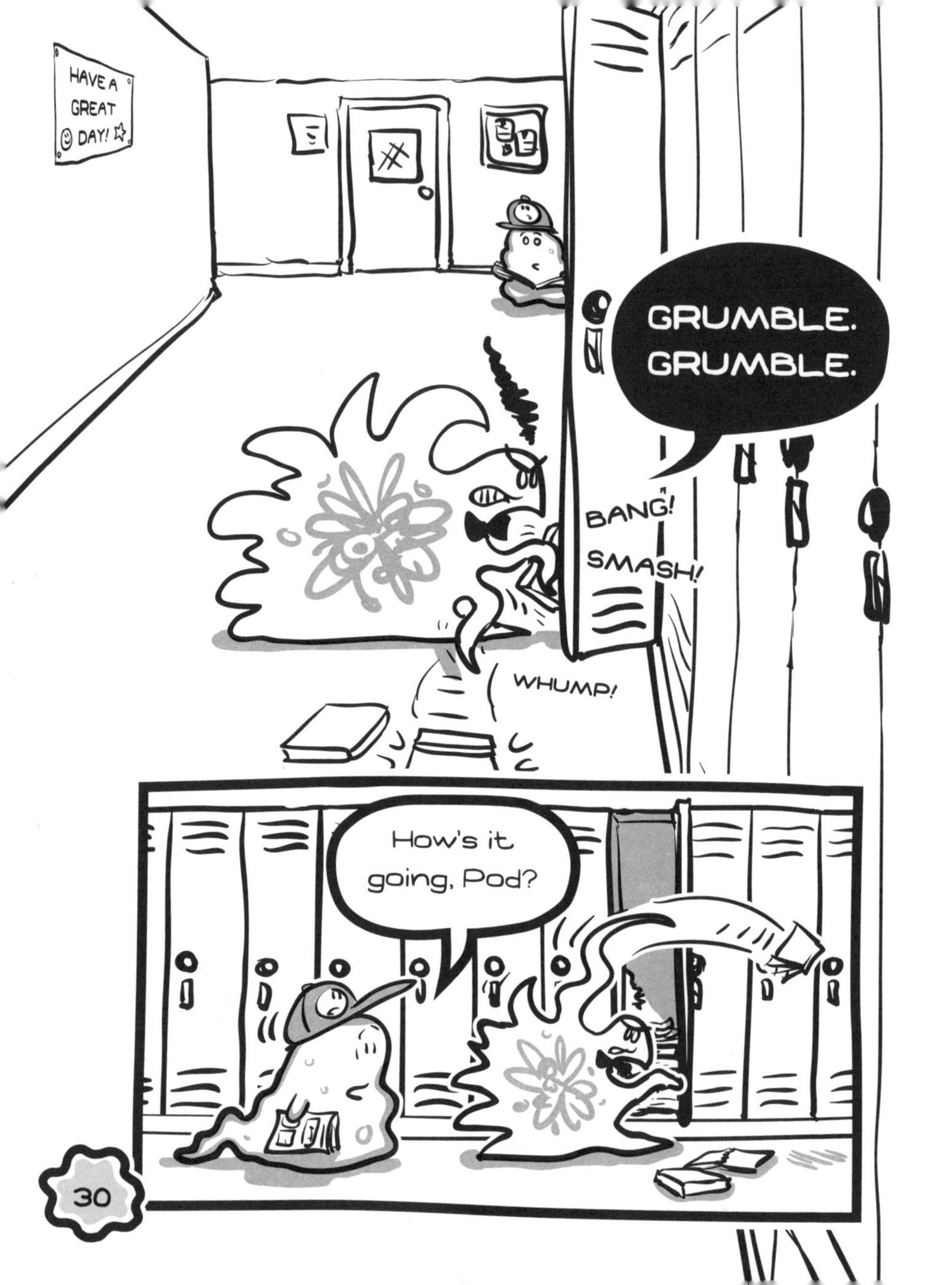
HAVE A GREAT DAY!
GRUMBLE. GRUMBLE.
BANG!
SMASH!
WHUMP!
How's it going, Pod?

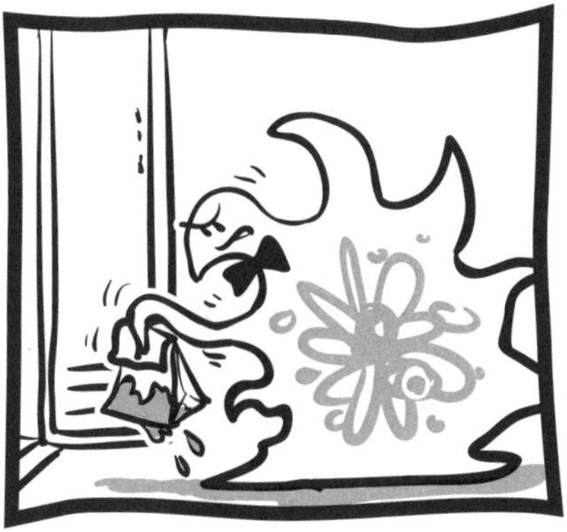

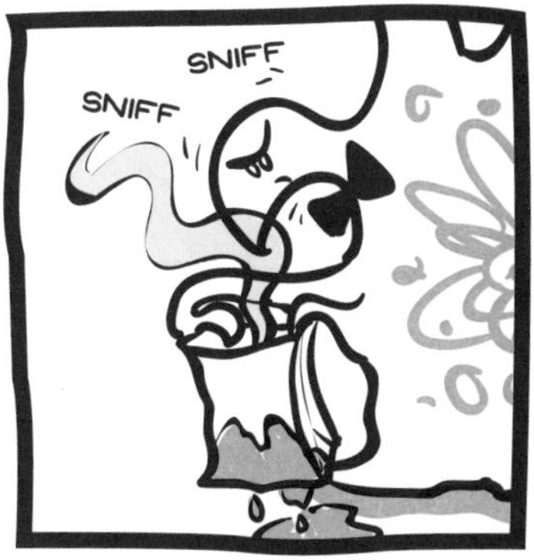
SNIFF
SNIFF

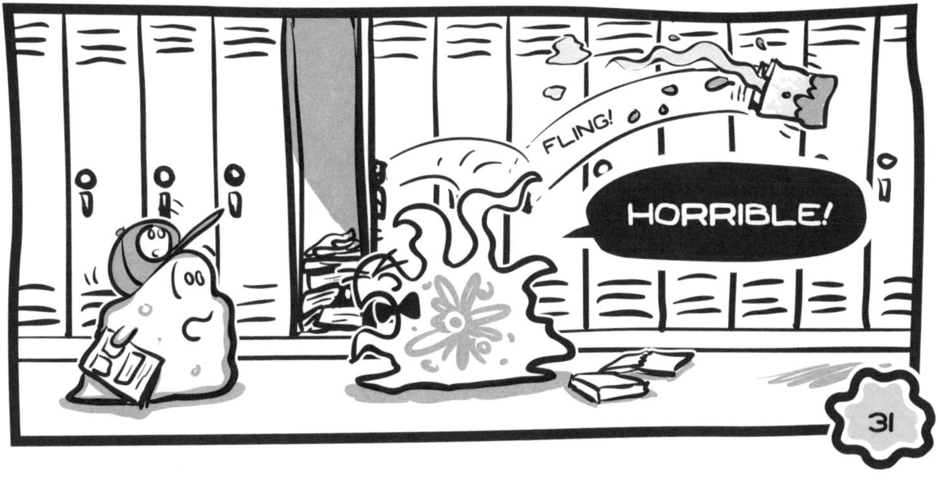
FLING!
HORRIBLE!

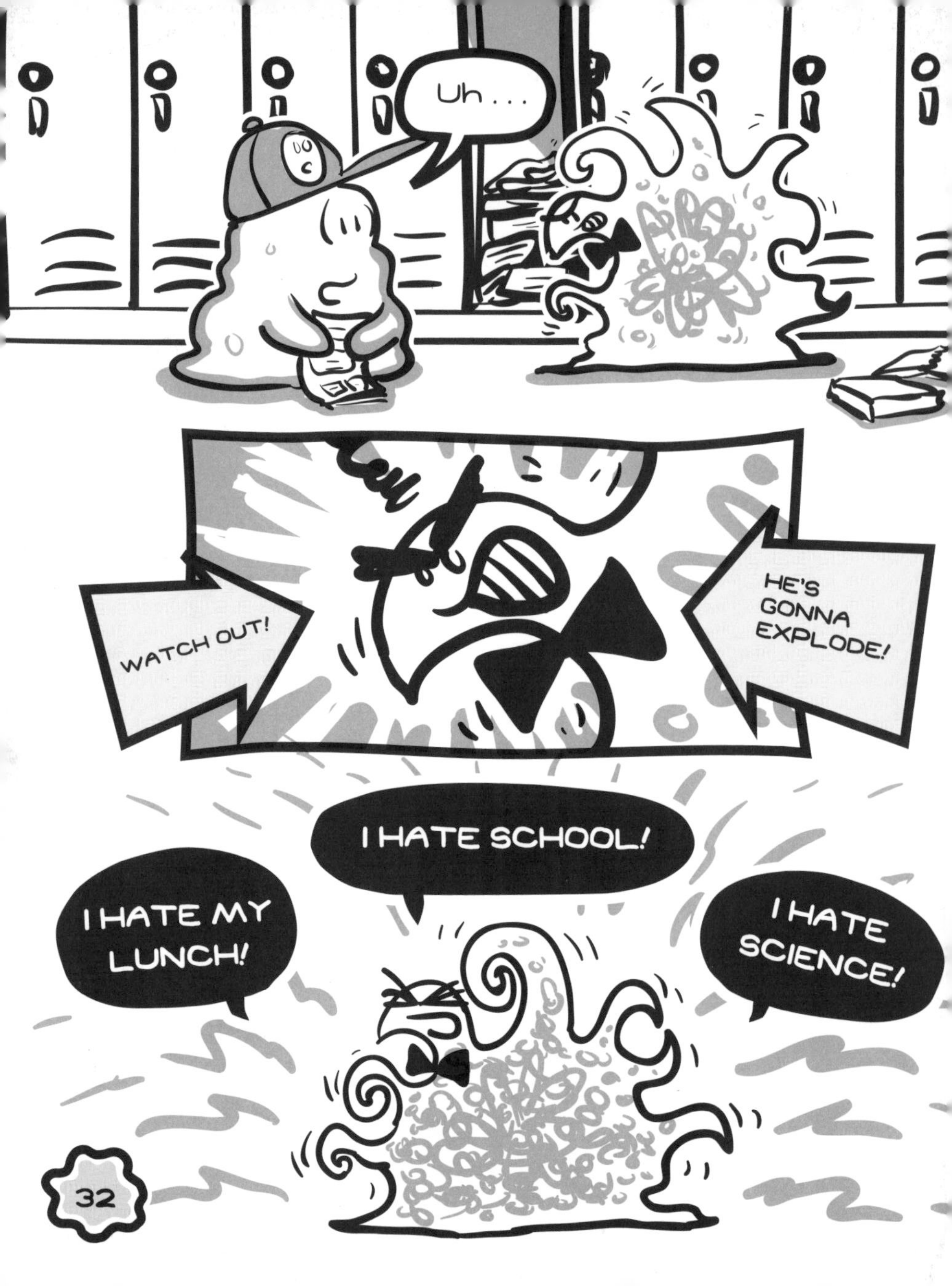
Uh . . .
WATCH OUT!
HE'S GONNA EXPLODE!
I HATE SCHOOL!
I HATE MY LUNCH!
I HATE SCIENCE!

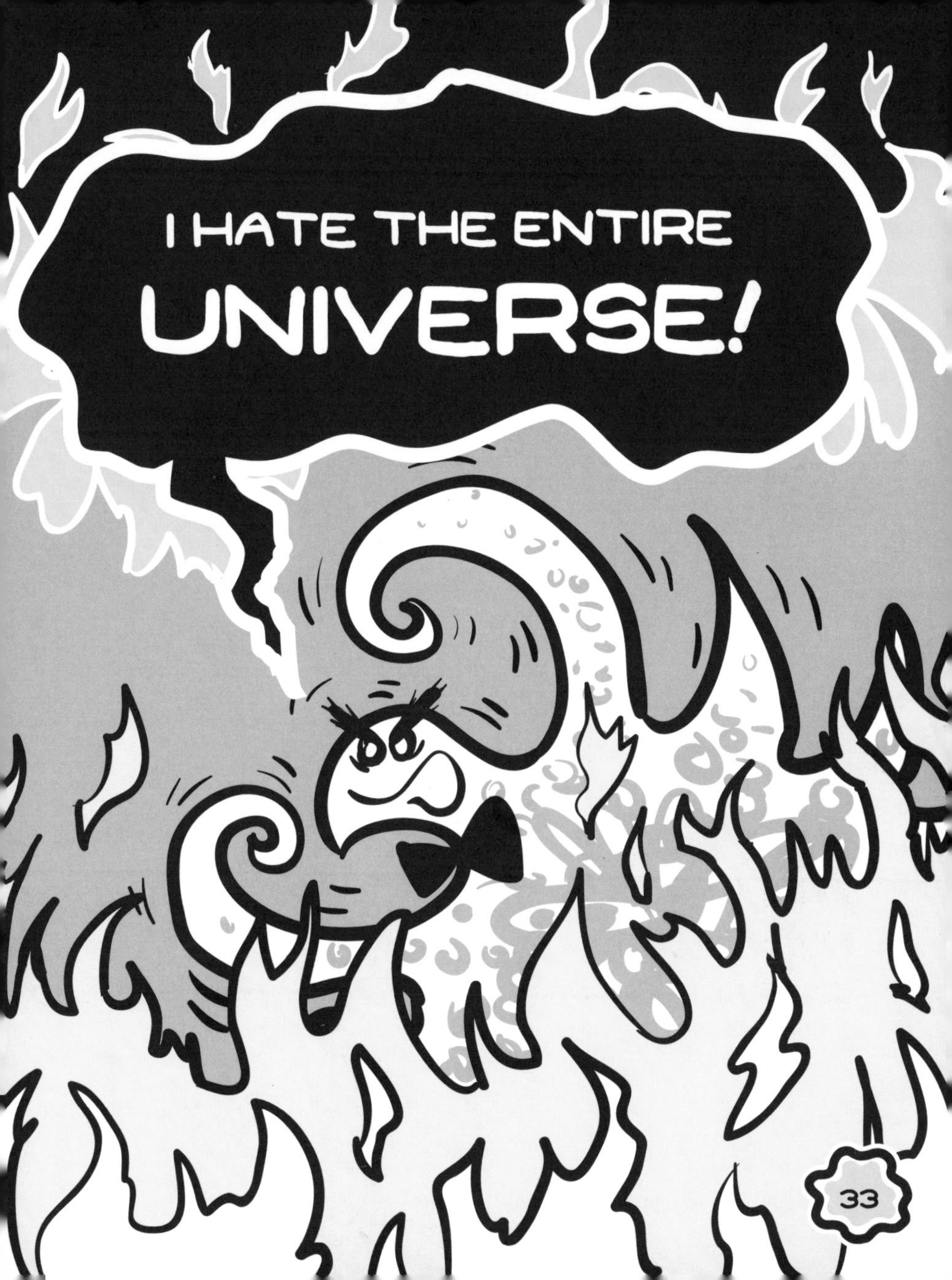
I HATE THE ENTIRE
UNIVERSE!

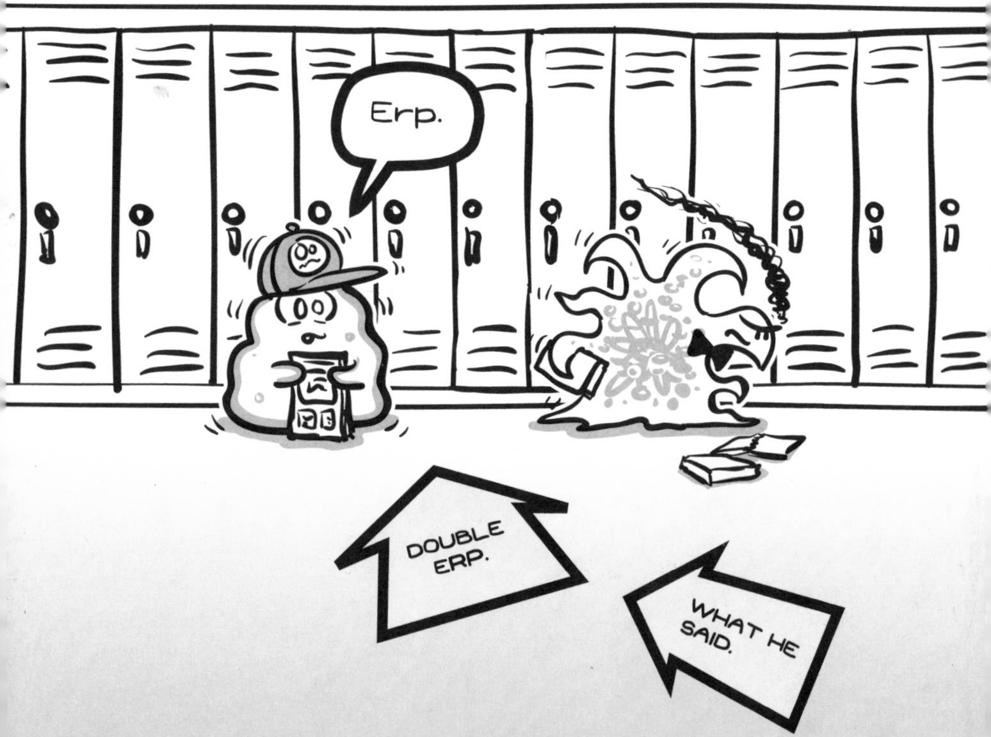
Erp.
DOUBLE ERP.
WHAT HE SAID.

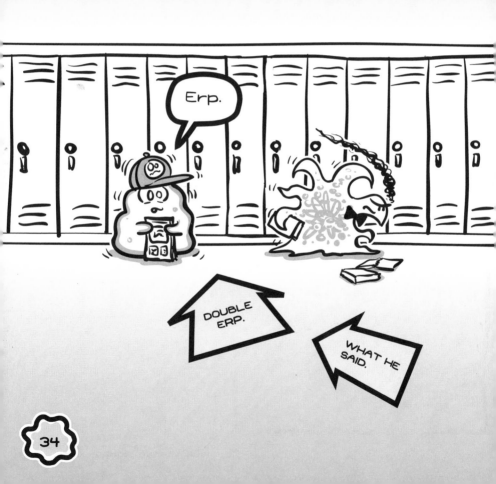

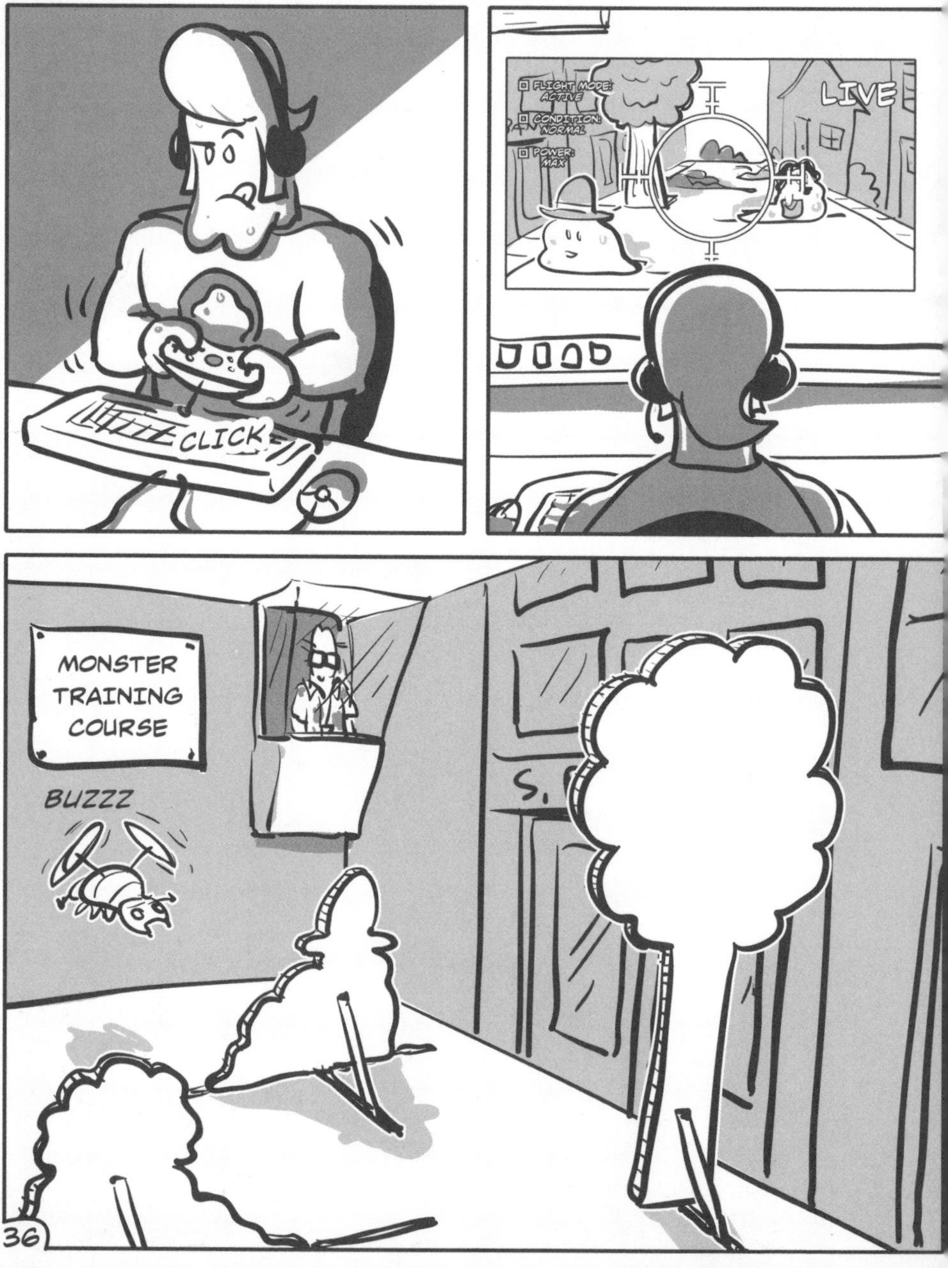
CLICK
FLIGHT MODE: ACTIVE
CONDITION: NORMAL
POWER: MAX
LIVE
MONSTER TRAINING COURSE
BUZZZ

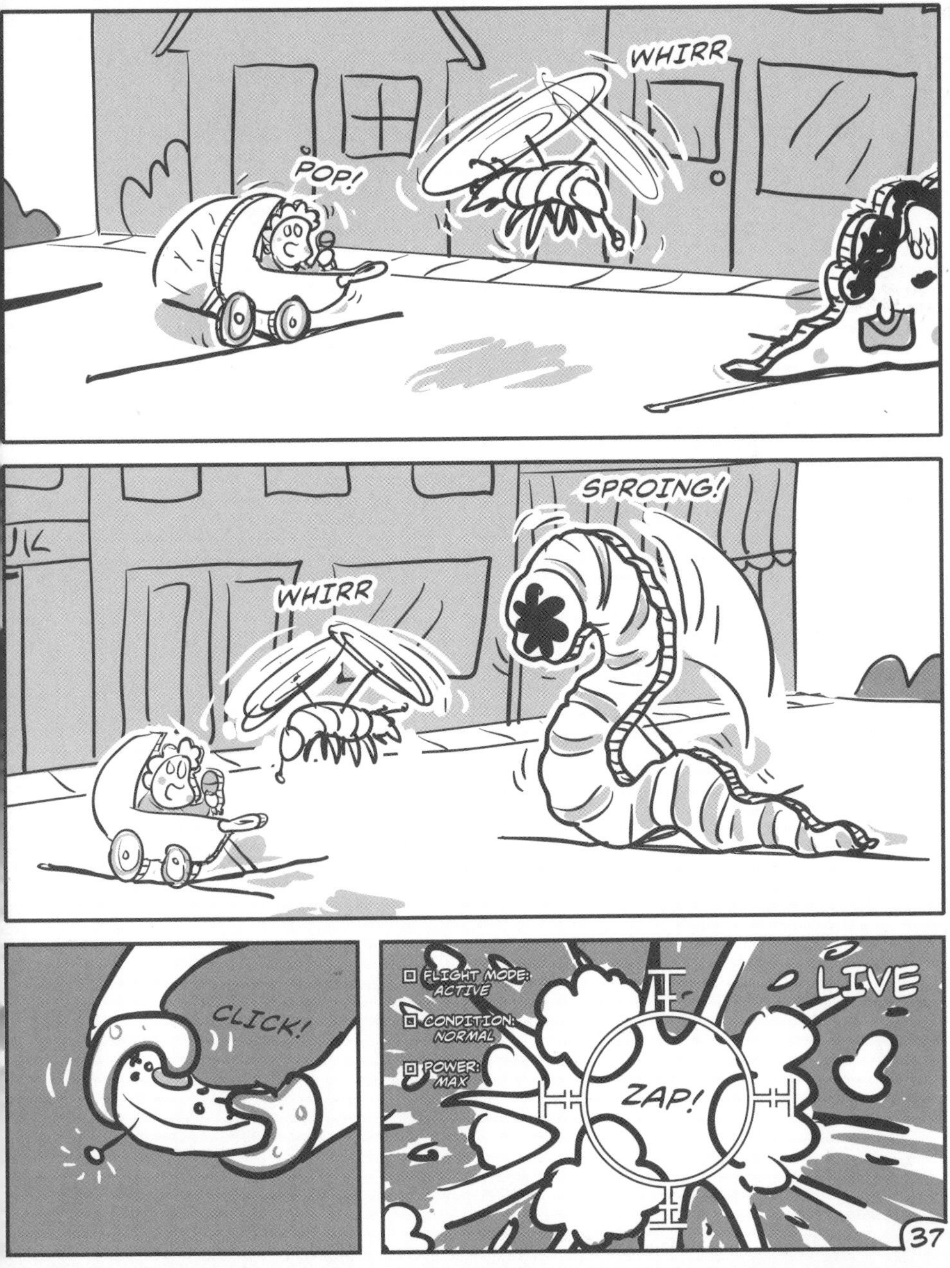
WHIRR
POP!
SPROING!
WHIRR
CLICK!
FLIGHT MODE: ACTIVE
CONDITION: NORMAL
POWER: MAX
LIVE
ZAP!

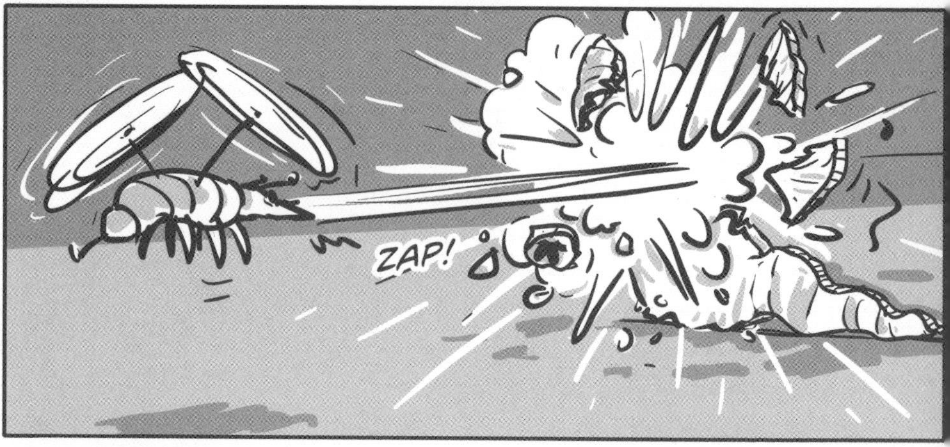
ZAP!

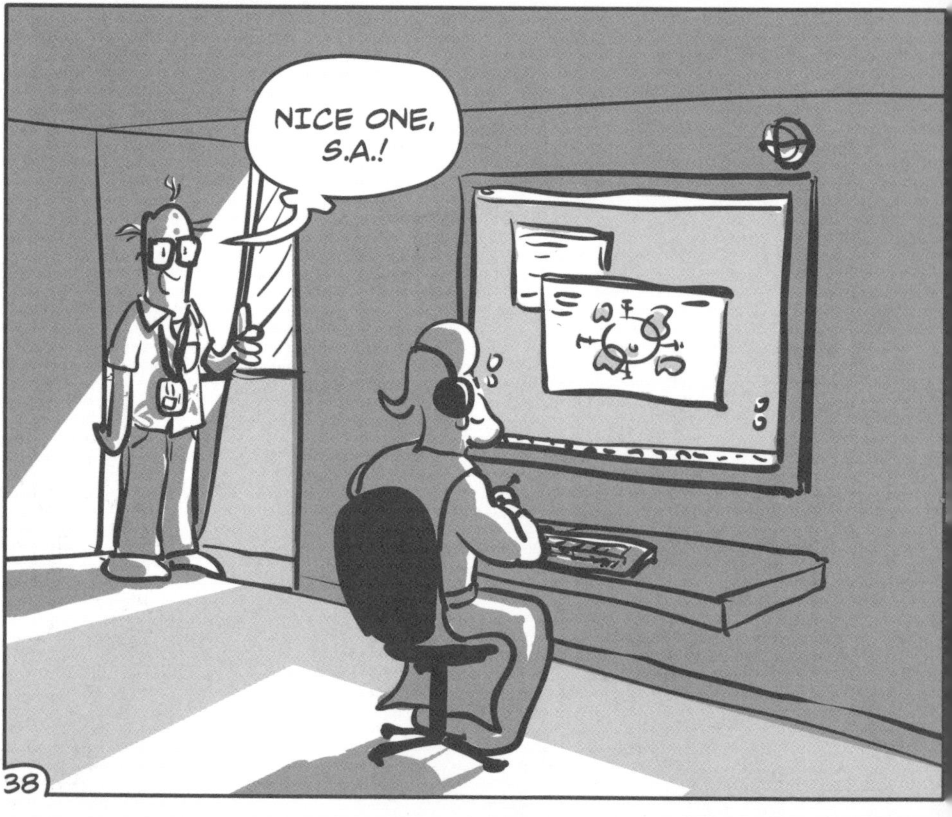
NICE ONE, S.A.!

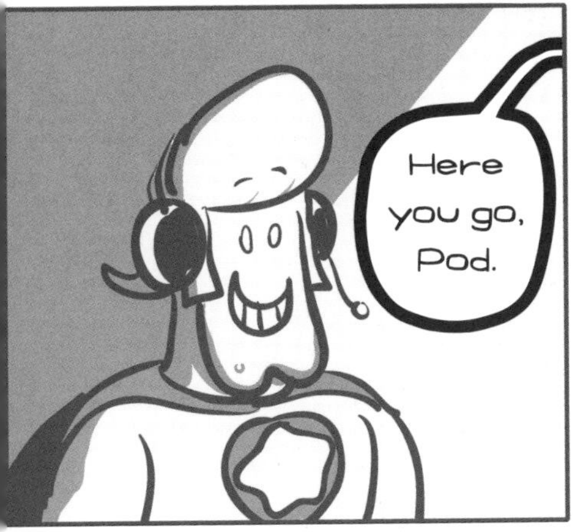
Here you go, Pod.

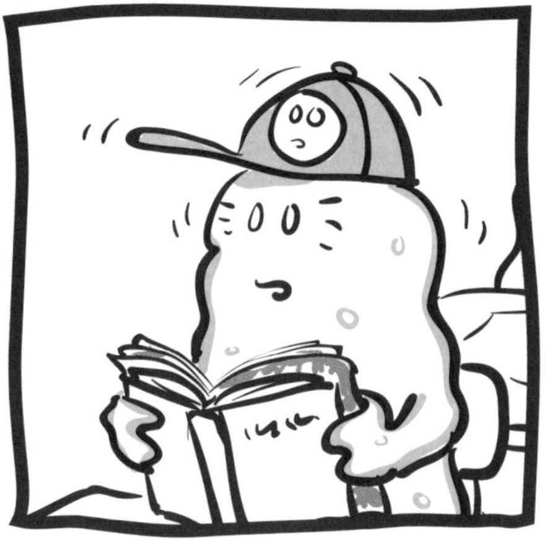

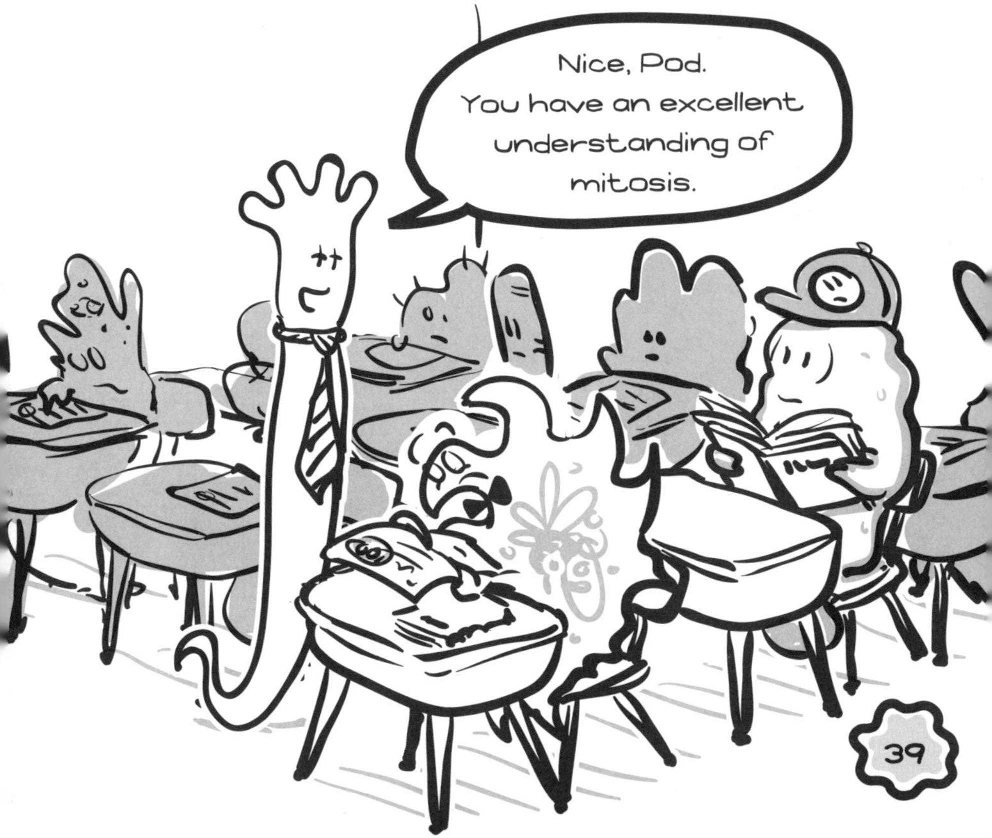
Nice, Pod. You have an excellent understanding of mitosis.

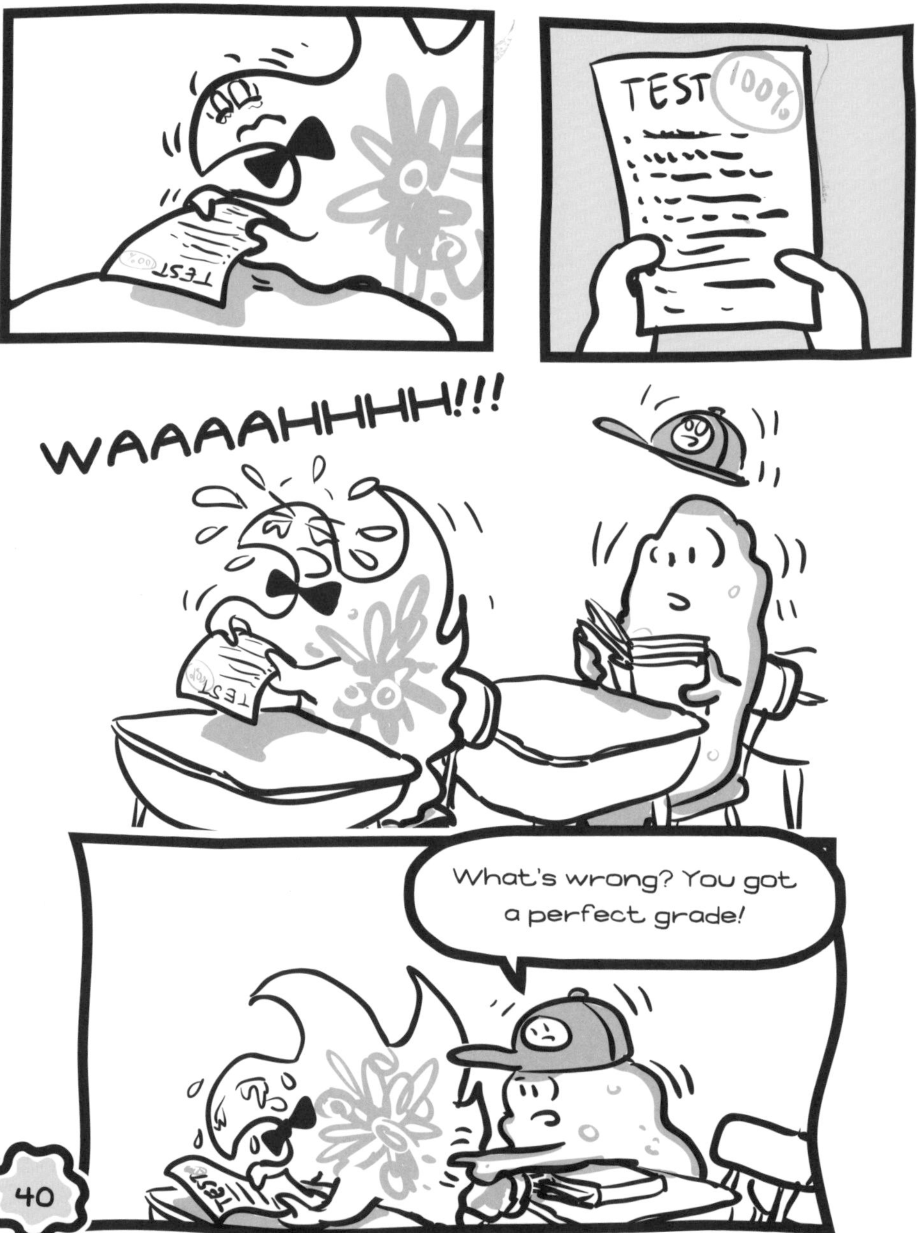
TEST
100%
TEST
100%
WAAAAHHHH!!!
What's wrong? You got a perfect grade!

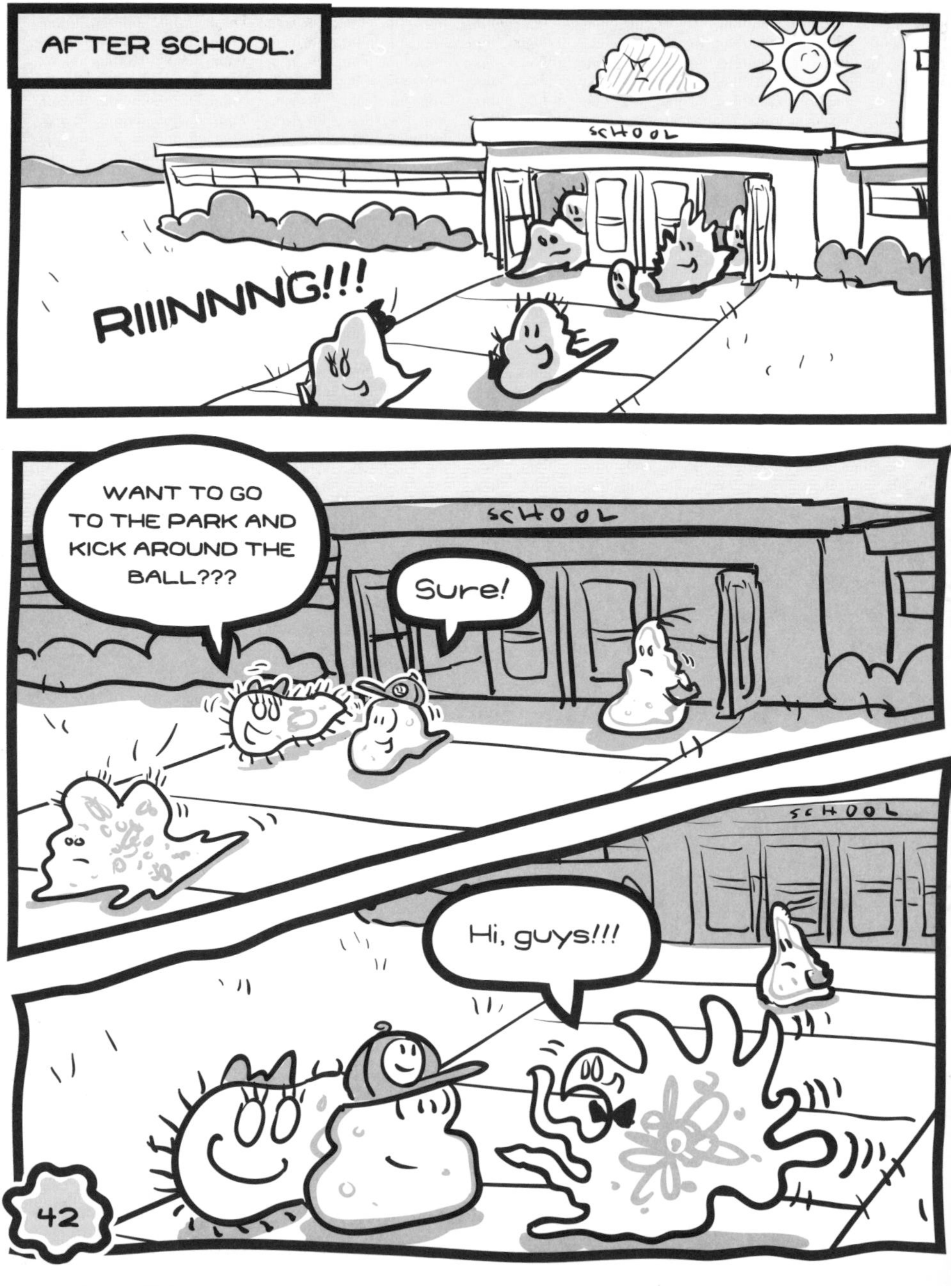
AFTER SCHOOL.
SCHOOL
RIIINNNG!!!
SCHOOL
WANT TO GO TO THE PARK AND KICK AROUND THE BALL???
Sure!
SCHOOL
Hi, guys!!!

43

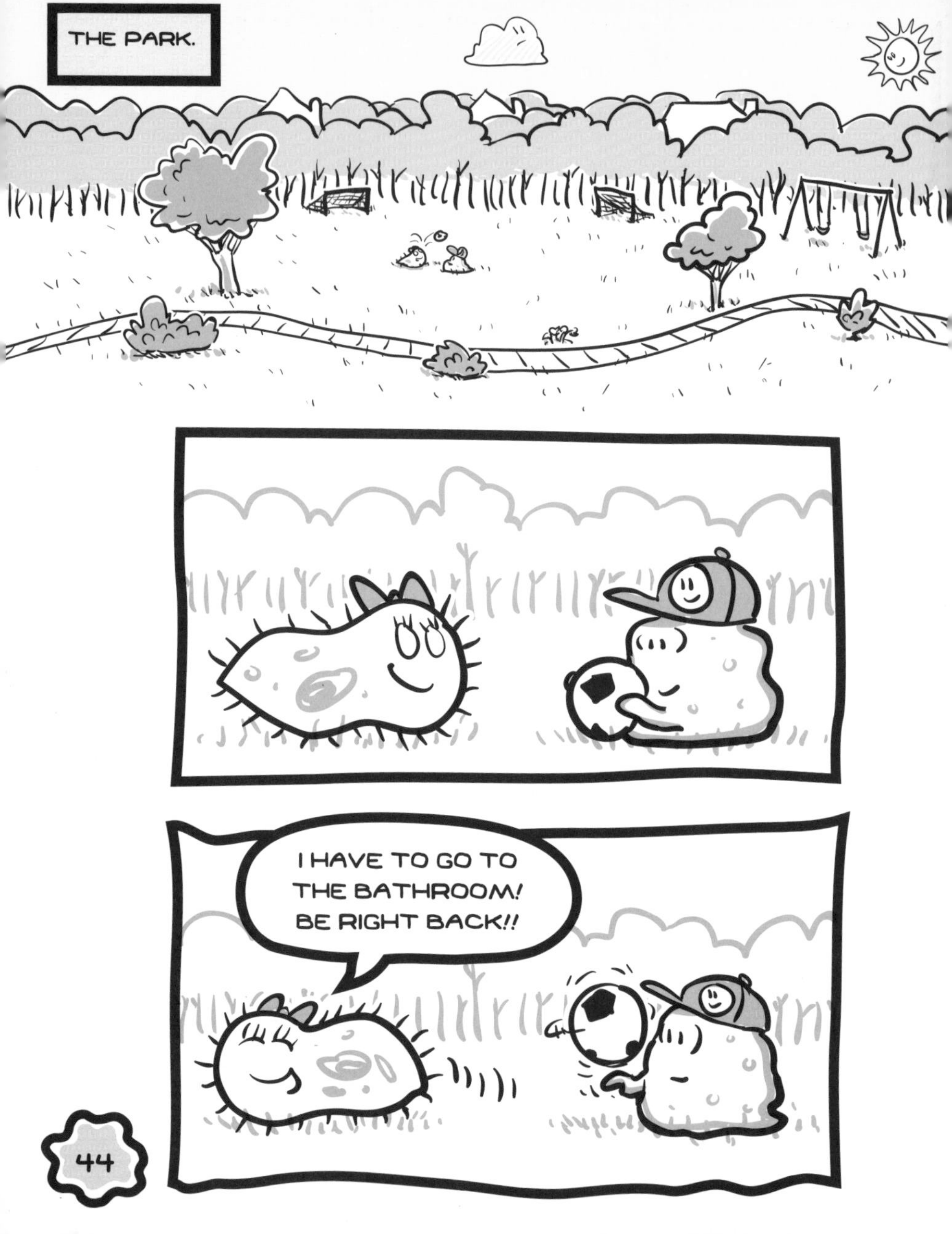
THE PARK.
I HAVE TO GO TO THE BATHROOM! BE RIGHT BACK!!

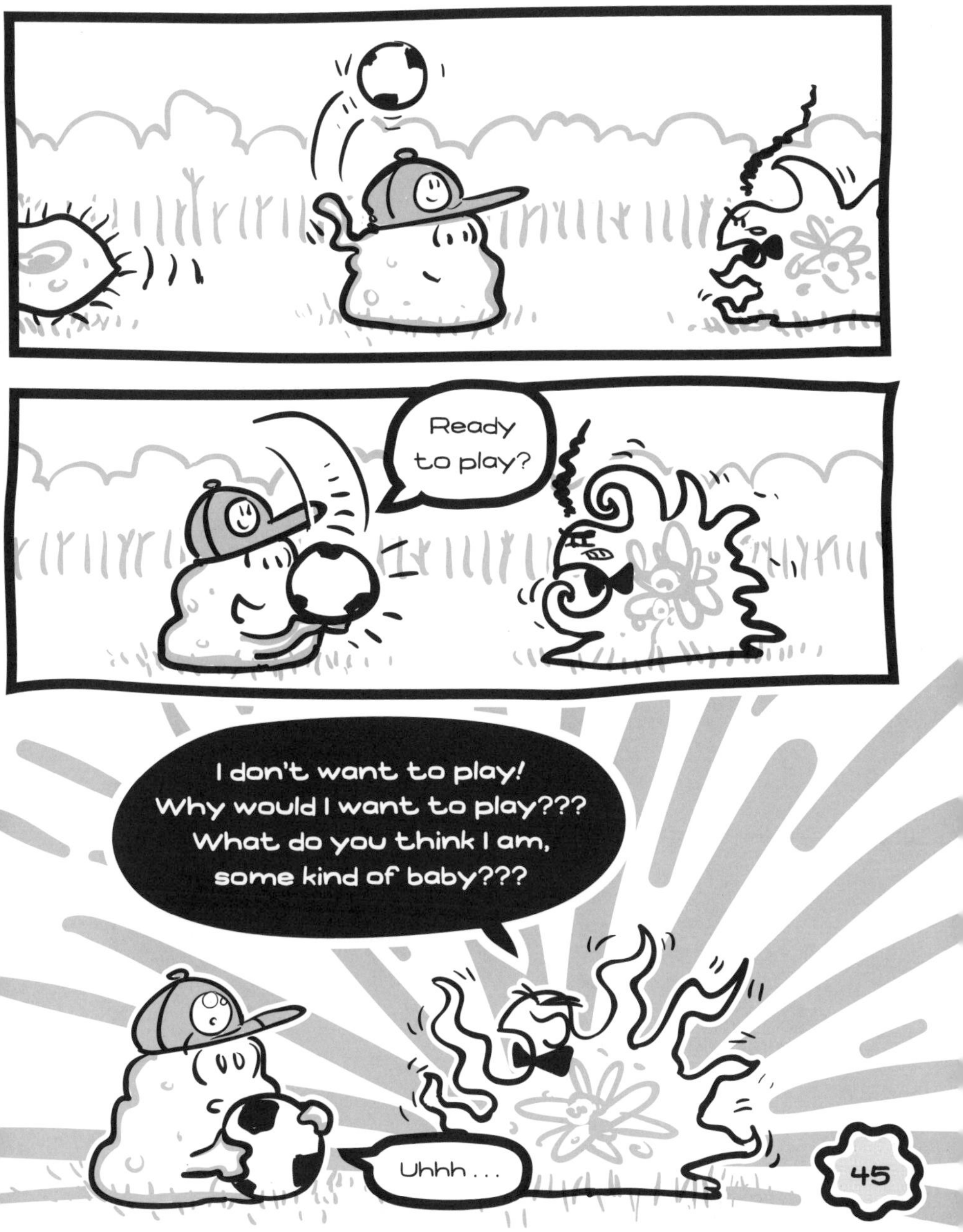
Ready to play?
I don't want to play! Why would I want to play??? What do you think I am, some kind of baby???
Uhhh . . .

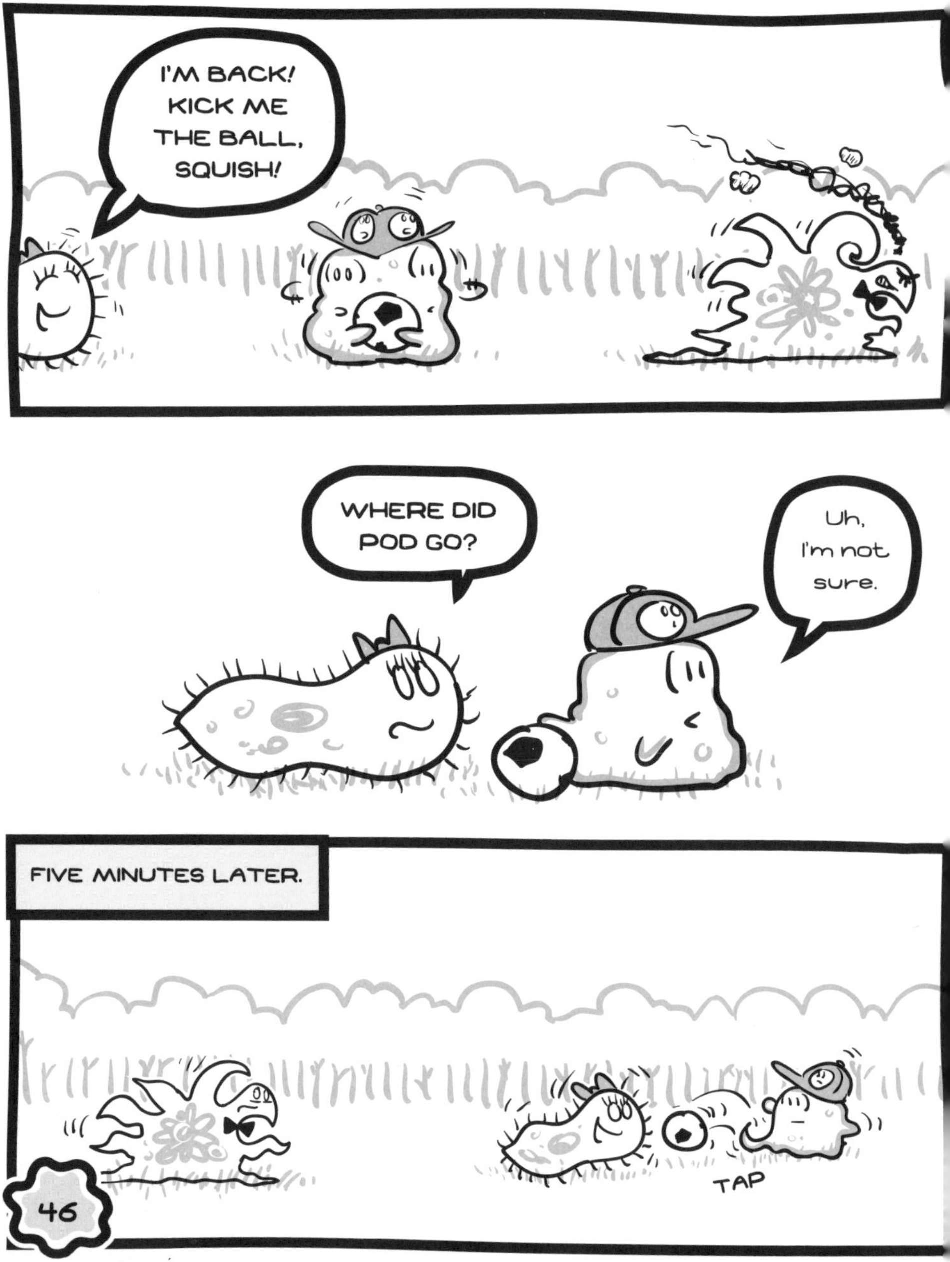
I'M BACK! KICK ME THE BALL, SQUISH!
WHERE DID POD GO?
Uh, I'm not sure.
FIVE MINUTES LATER.
TAP

SNIFF!

QUIVER!

BLINK!

47

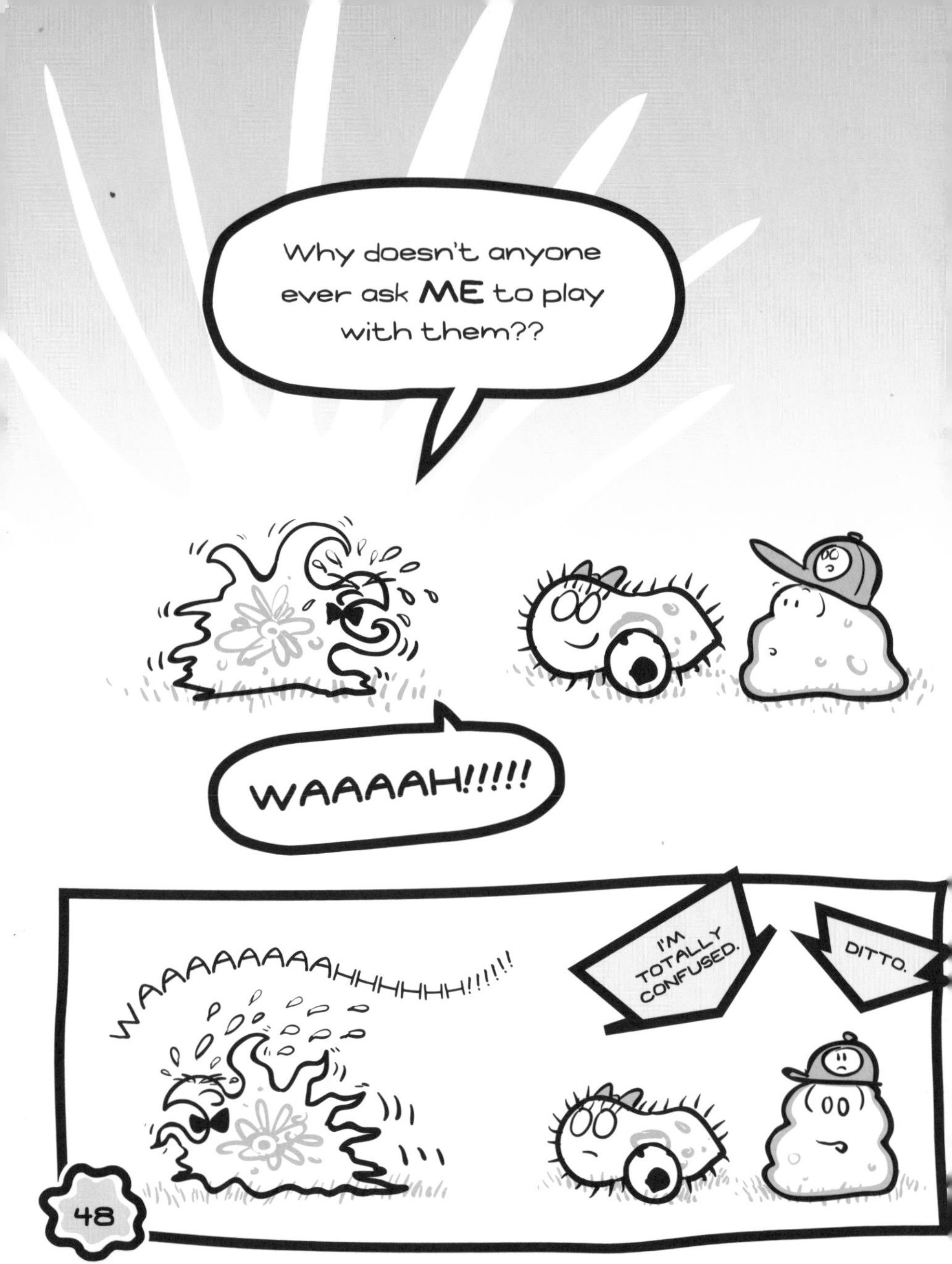
Why doesn't anyone ever ask **ME** to play with them??
WAAAAH!!!!!
WAAAAAAAAAHHHHHHH!!!!!
I'M TOTALLY CONFUSED.
DITTO.

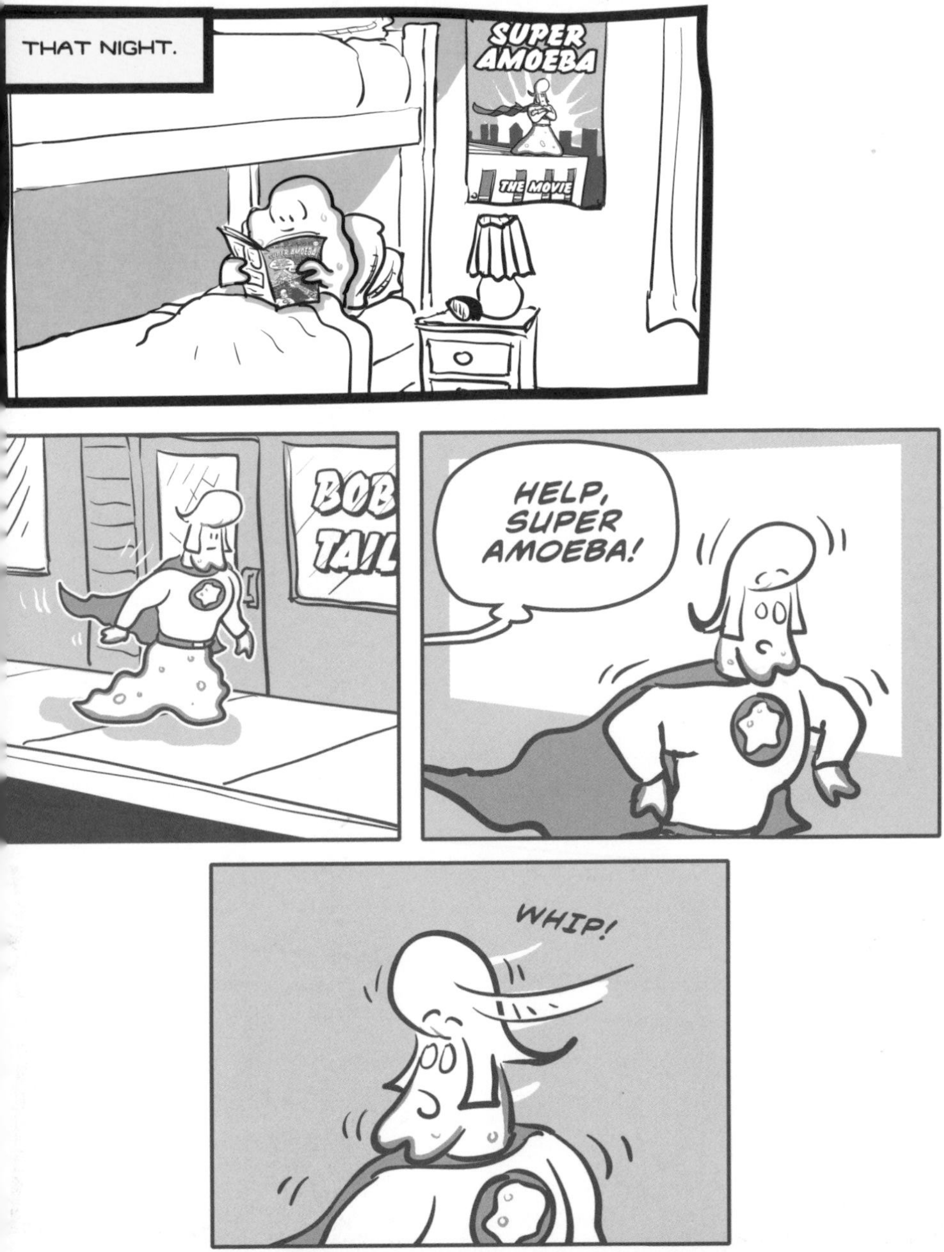
THAT NIGHT.
SUPER AMOEBA
THE MOVIE
SUPER AMOEBA
BOB
TAIL
HELP, SUPER AMOEBA!
WHIP!

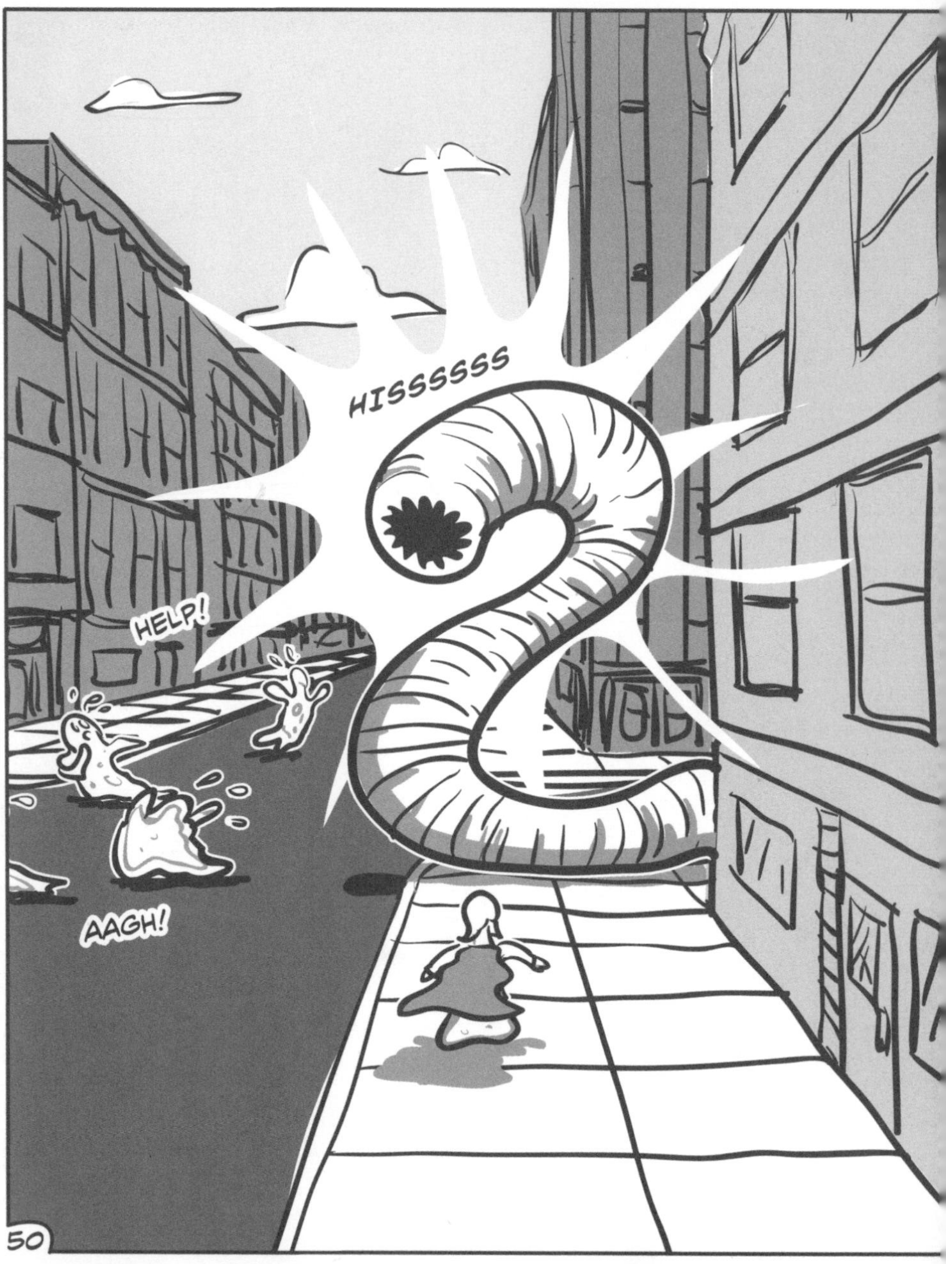
HISSSSSS
HELP!
AAGH!

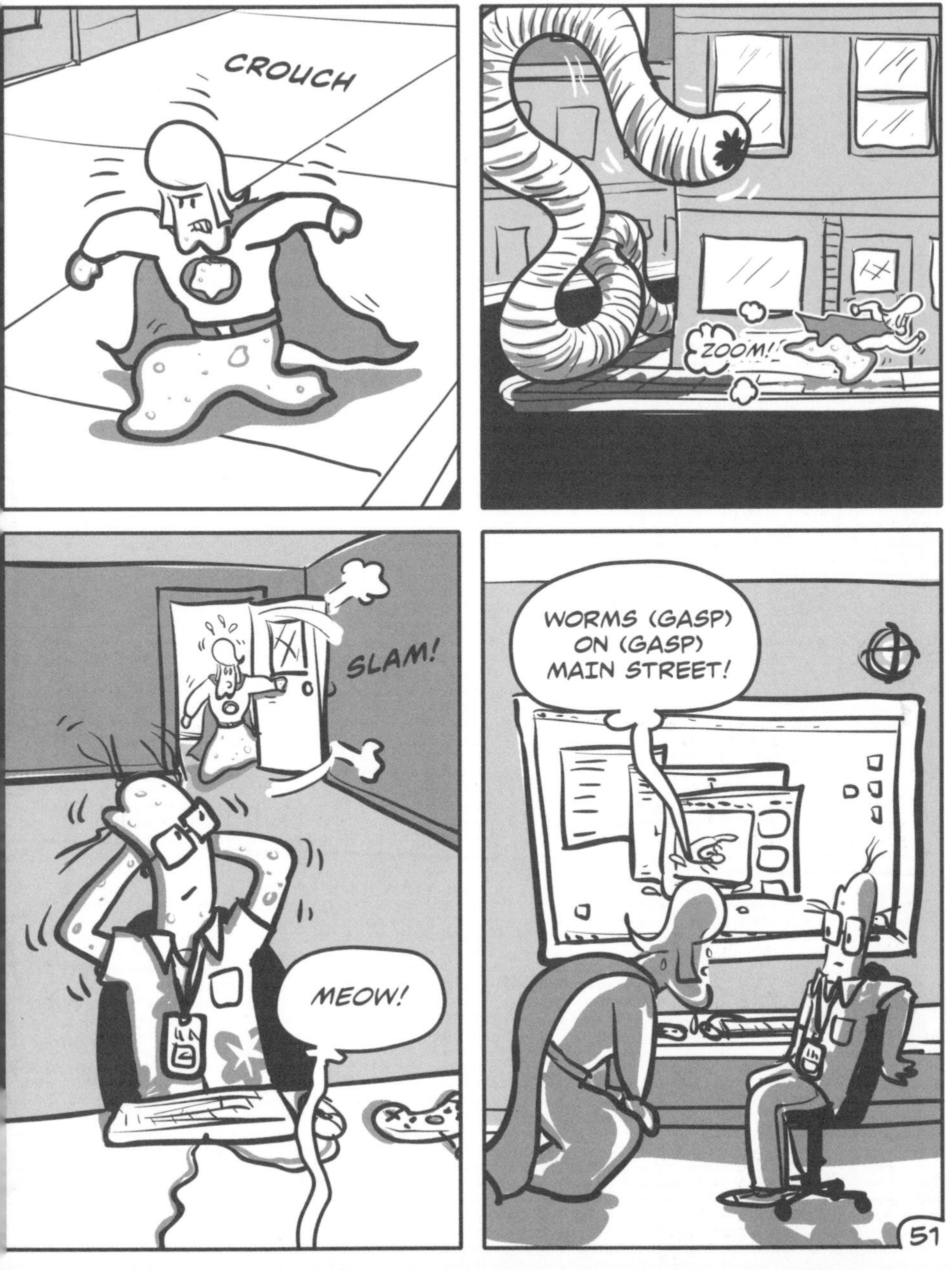
CROUCH
ZOOM!
SLAM!
MEOW!
WORMS (GASP) ON (GASP) MAIN STREET!

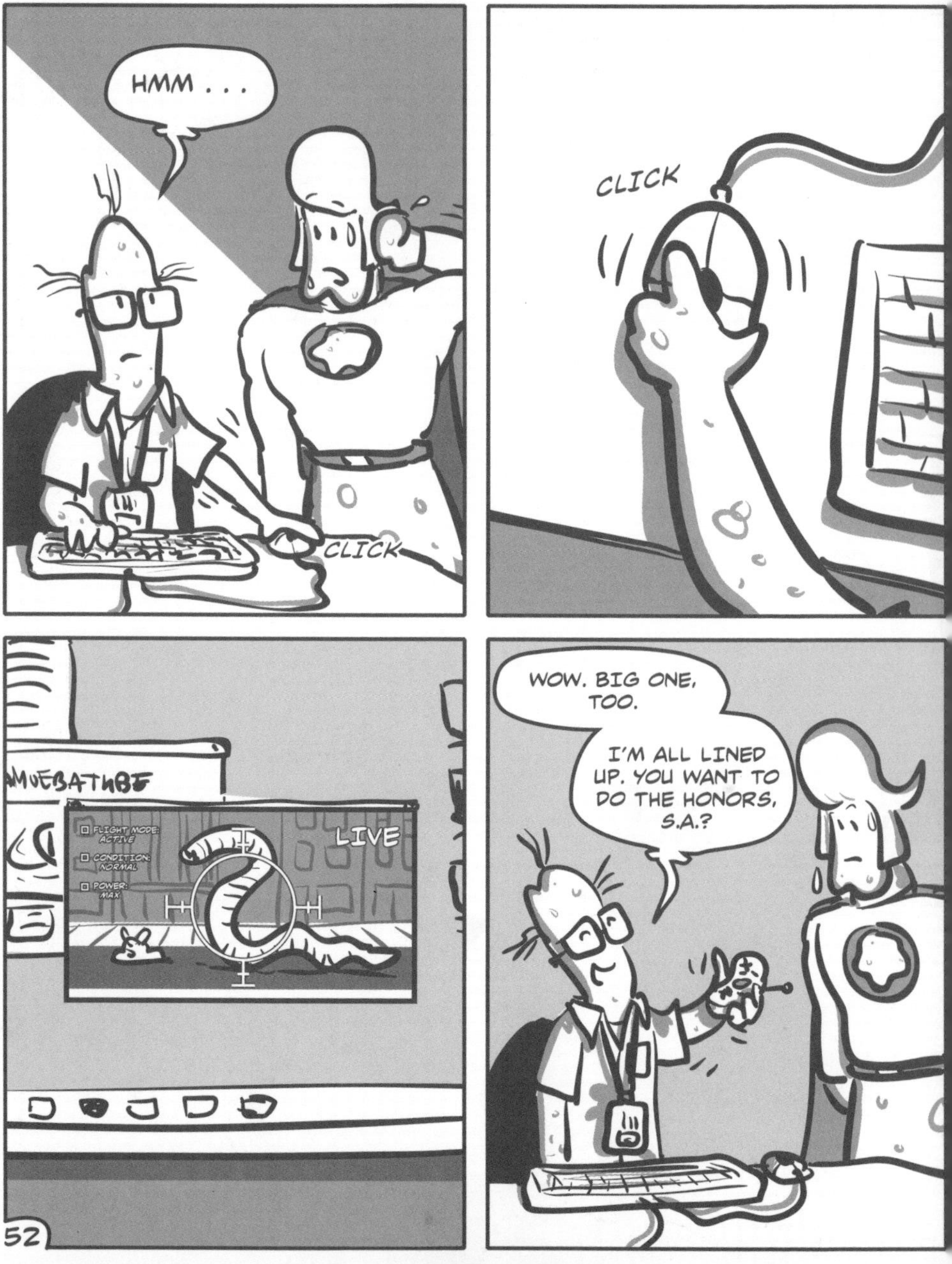
HMM . . .
CLICK
CLICK
FLIGHT MODE: ACTIVE
CONDITION: NORMAL
POWER: MAX
LIVE
WOW. BIG ONE, TOO.
I'M ALL LINED UP. YOU WANT TO DO THE HONORS, S.A.?

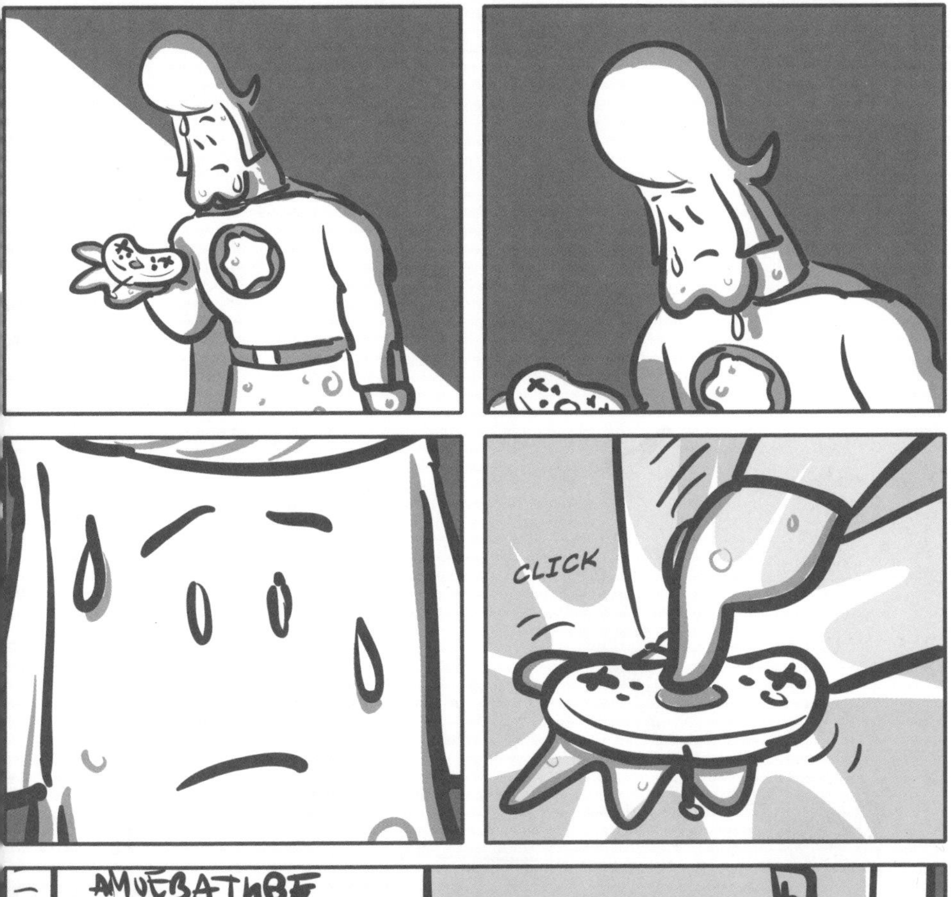
CLICK
FLIGHT MODE: ACTIVE
CONDITION: NORMAL
POWER: MAX
LIVE
ZAP!
SIZZLE!

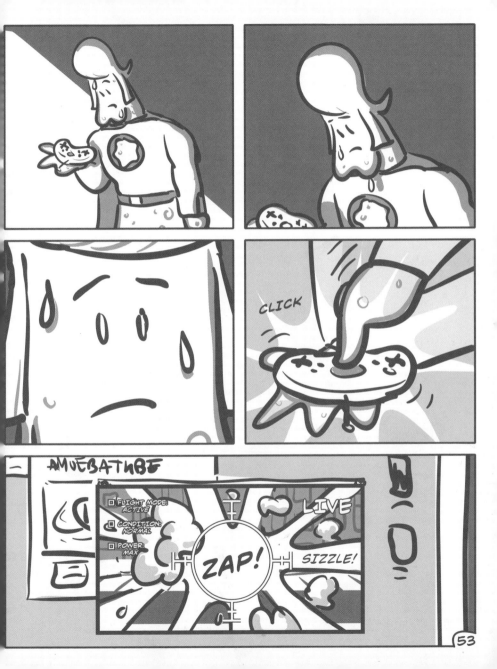

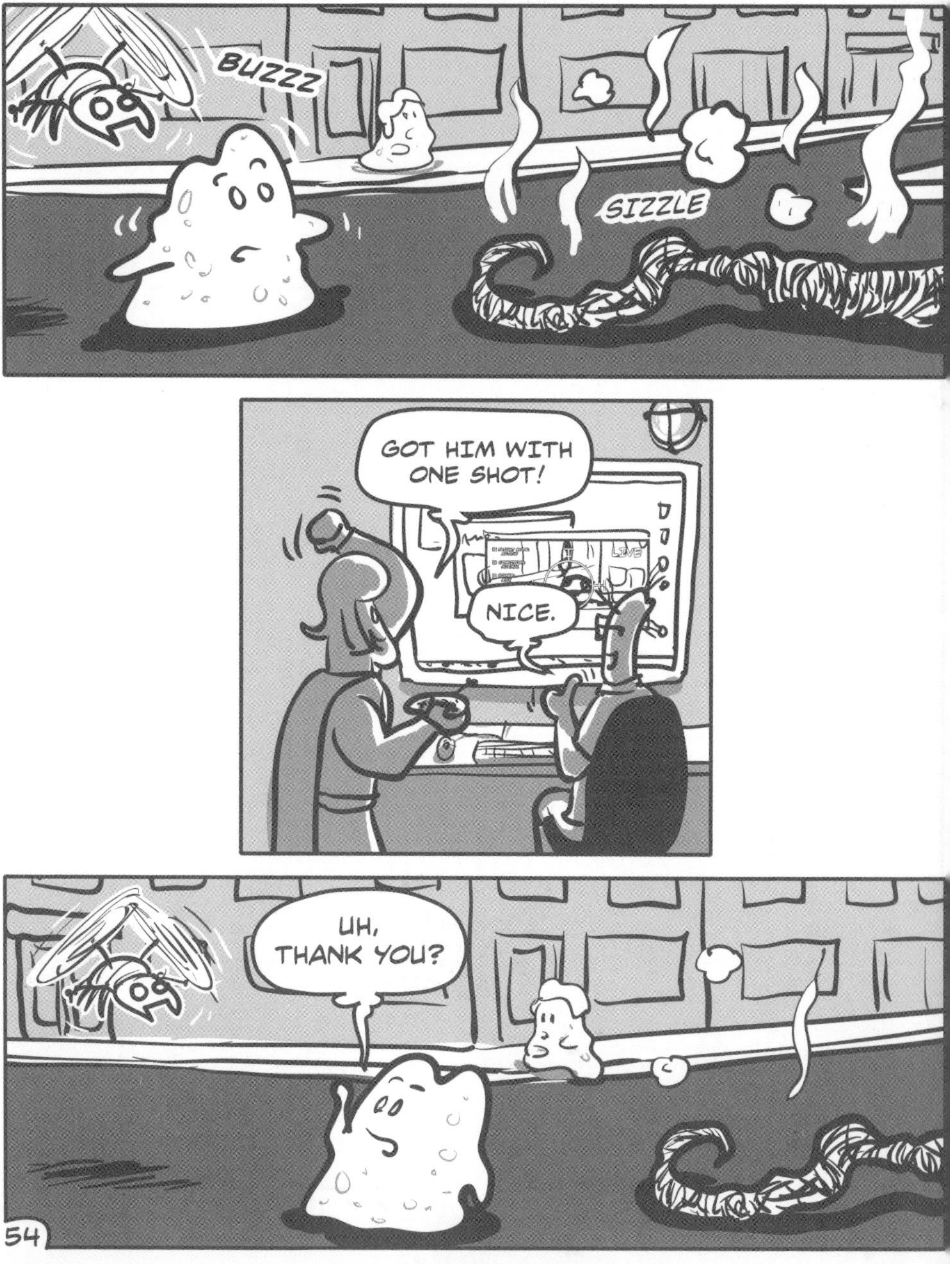
BUZZZ
SIZZLE
GOT HIM WITH ONE SHOT!
NICE.
UH, THANK YOU?

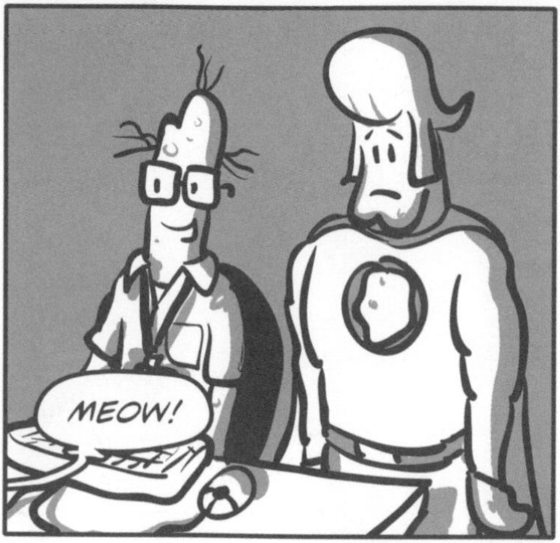
MEOW!

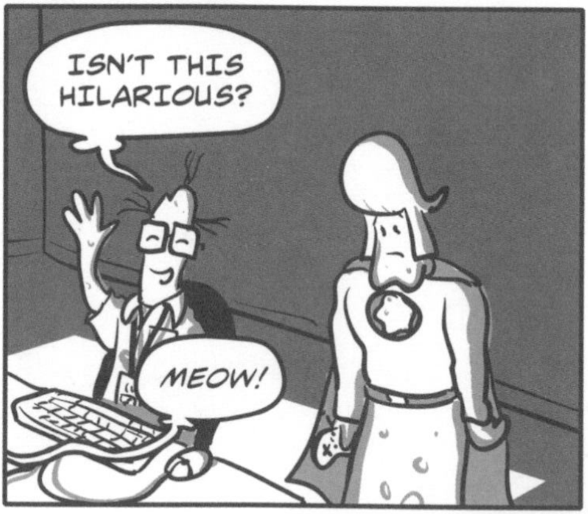
ISN'T THIS HILARIOUS?
MEOW!

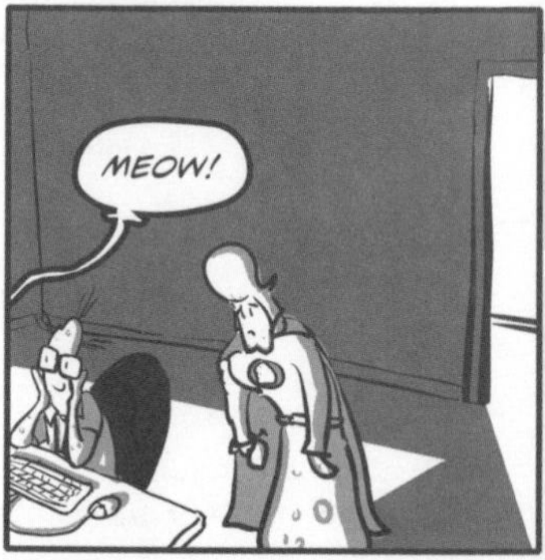
MEOW!

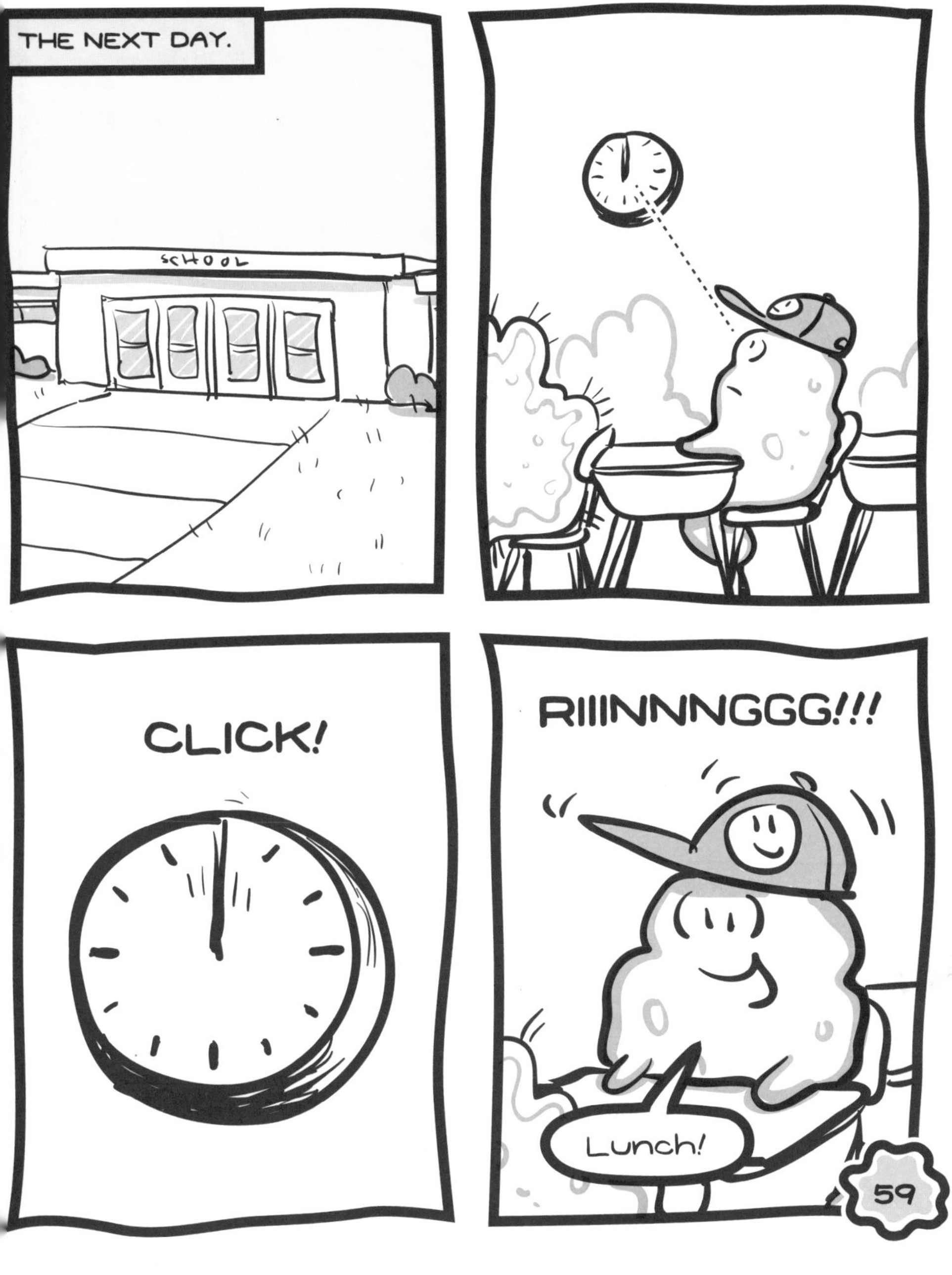
THE NEXT DAY.
SCHOOL
CLICK!
RIIINNNGGG!!!
Lunch!

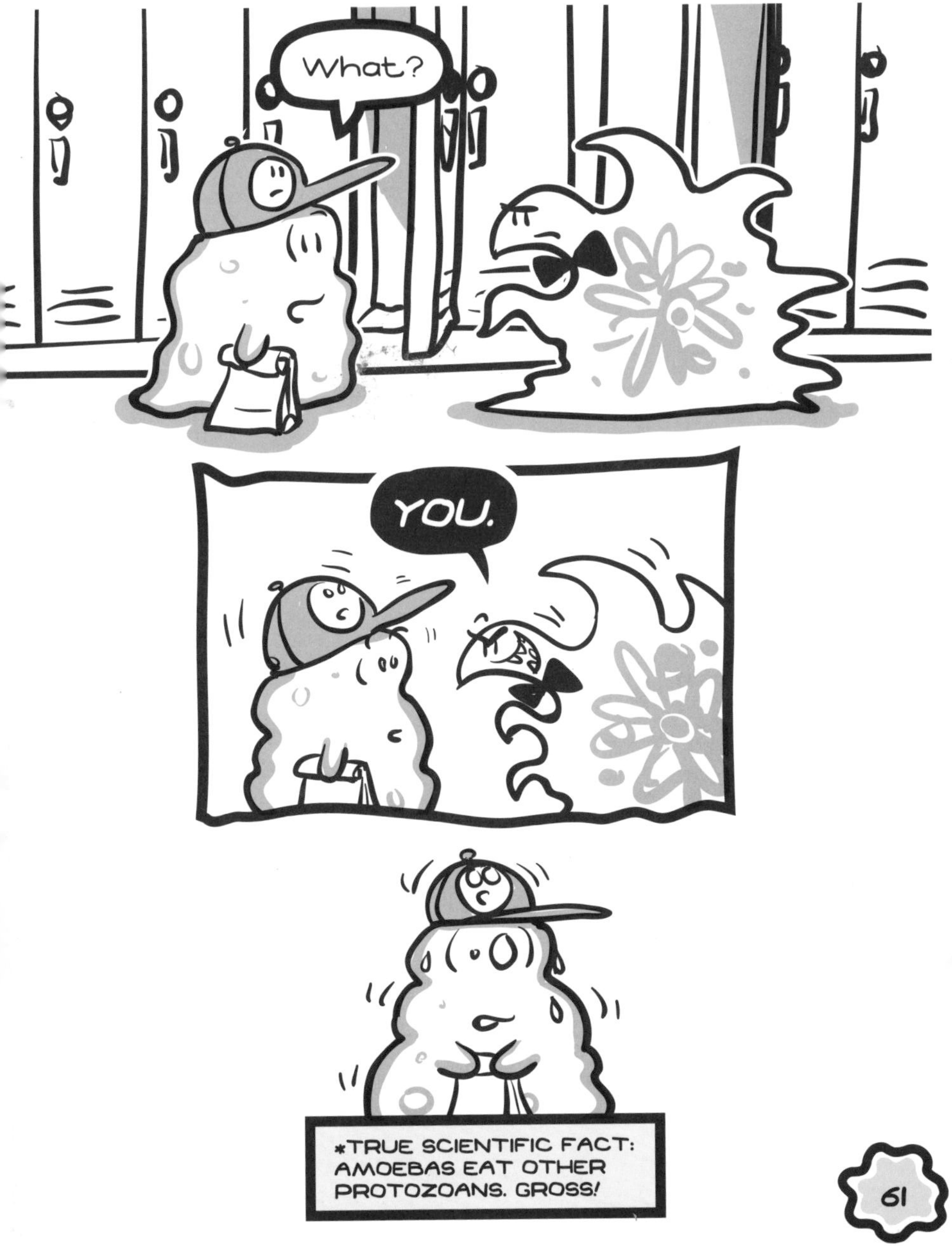
What?
YOU.
*TRUE SCIENTIFIC FACT: AMOEBAS EAT OTHER PROTOZOANS. GROSS!

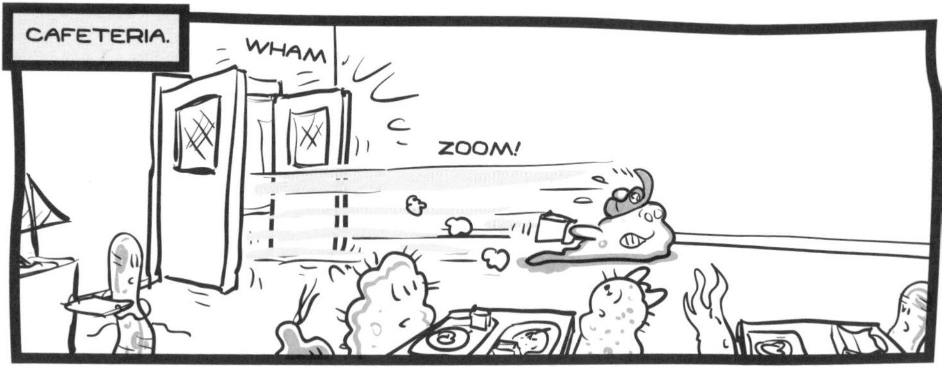
CAFETERIA.
WHAM
ZOOM!

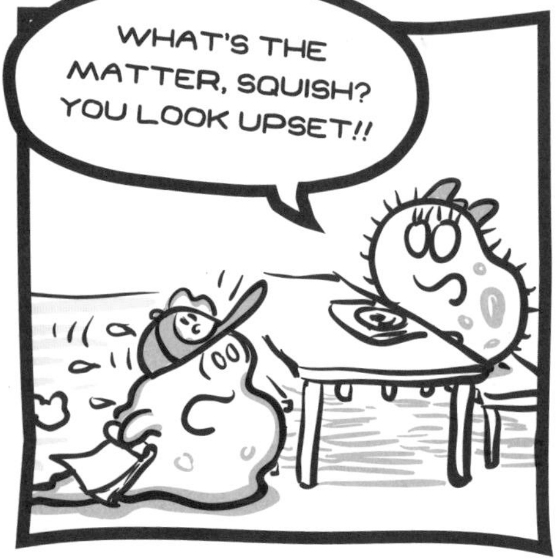
WHAT'S THE MATTER, SQUISH? YOU LOOK UPSET!!

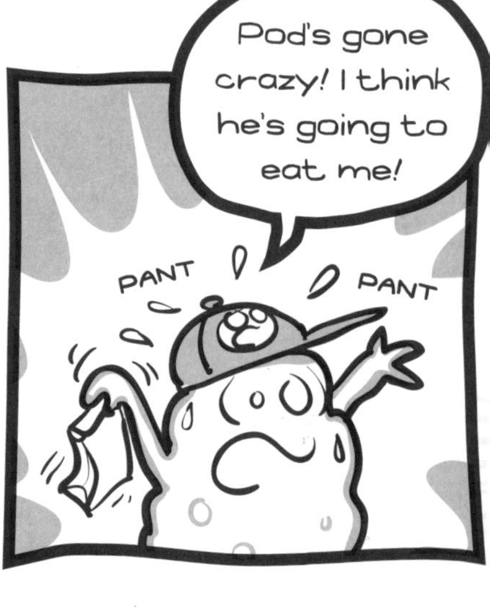
Pod's gone crazy! I think he's going to eat me!
PANT
PANT

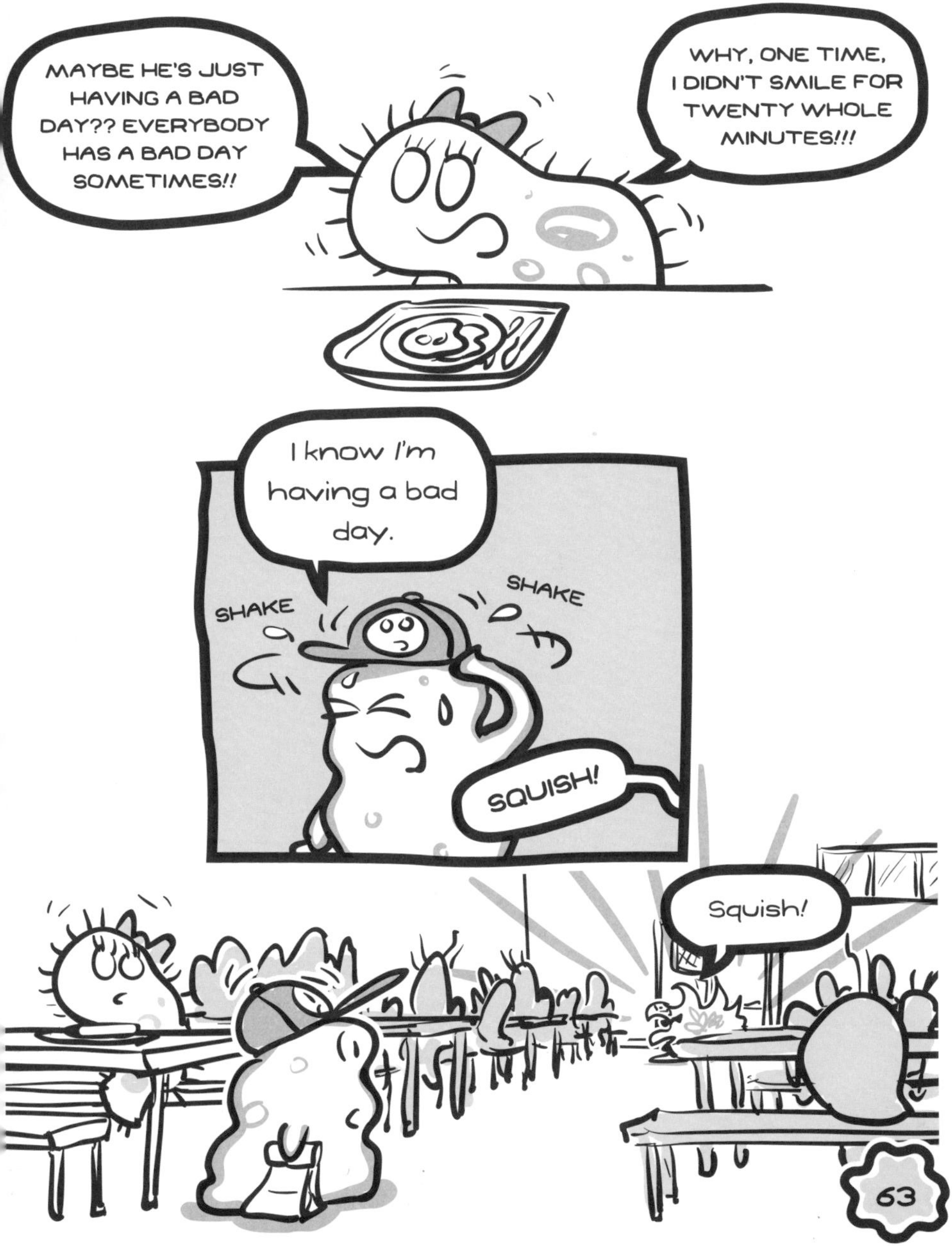

MAYBE HE'S JUST HAVING A BAD DAY?? EVERYBODY HAS A BAD DAY SOMETIMES!!
WHY, ONE TIME, I DIDN'T SMILE FOR TWENTY WHOLE MINUTES!!!
I know I'm having a bad day.
SHAKE
SHAKE
SQUISH!
Squish!

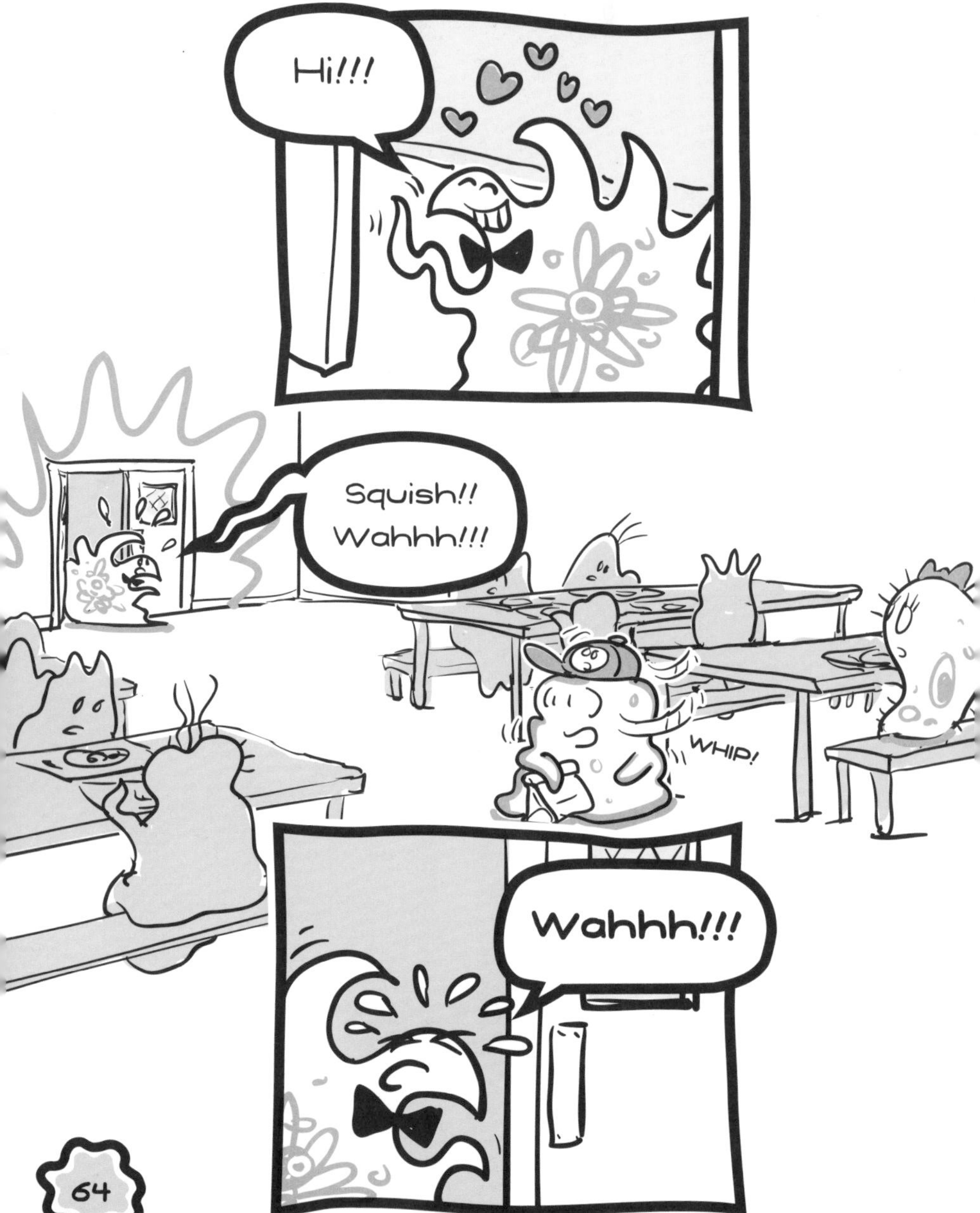
Hi!!!
Squish!!
Wahhh!!!
WHIP!
Wahhh!!!

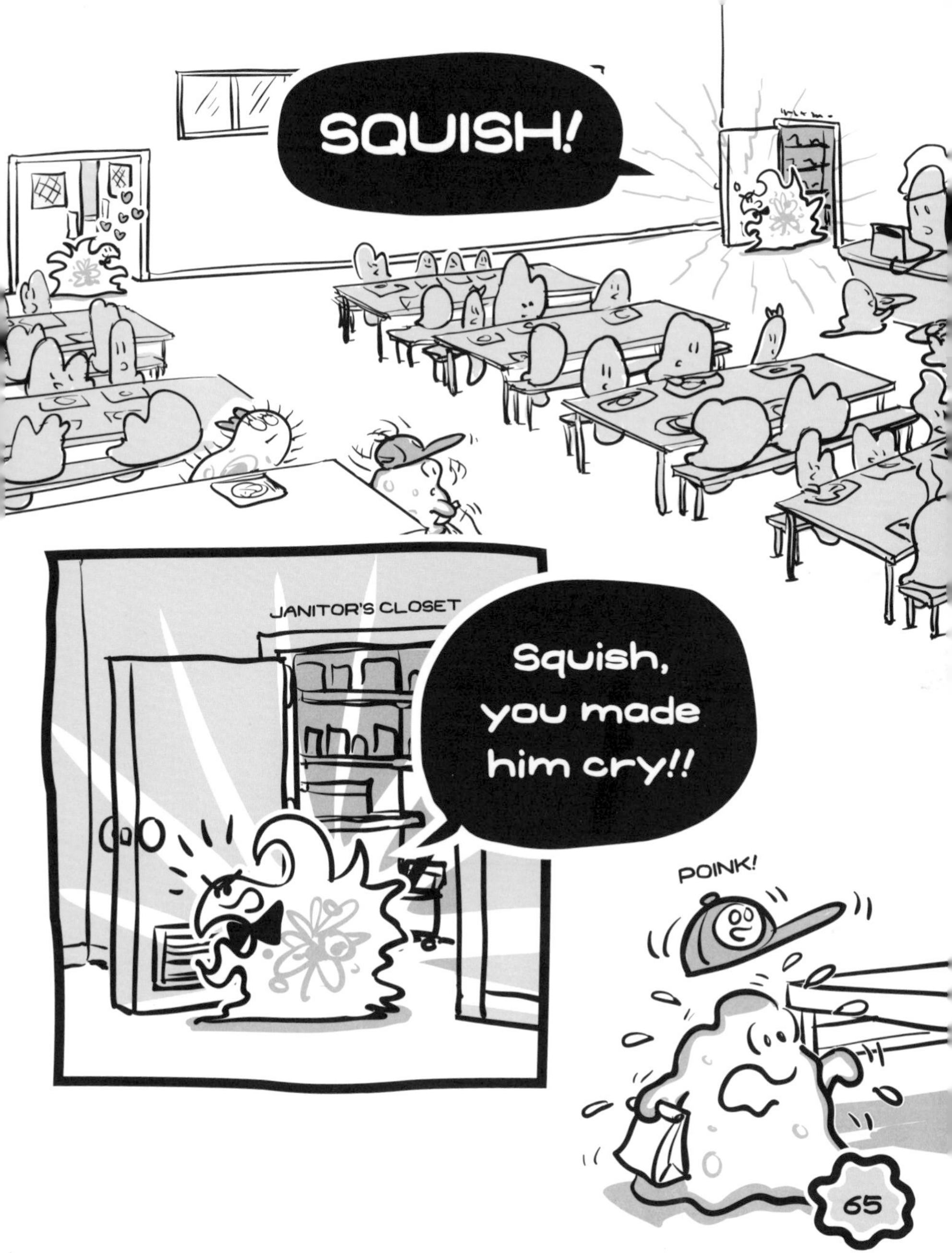
SQUISH!
JANITOR'S CLOSET
Squish, you made him cry!!
POINK!

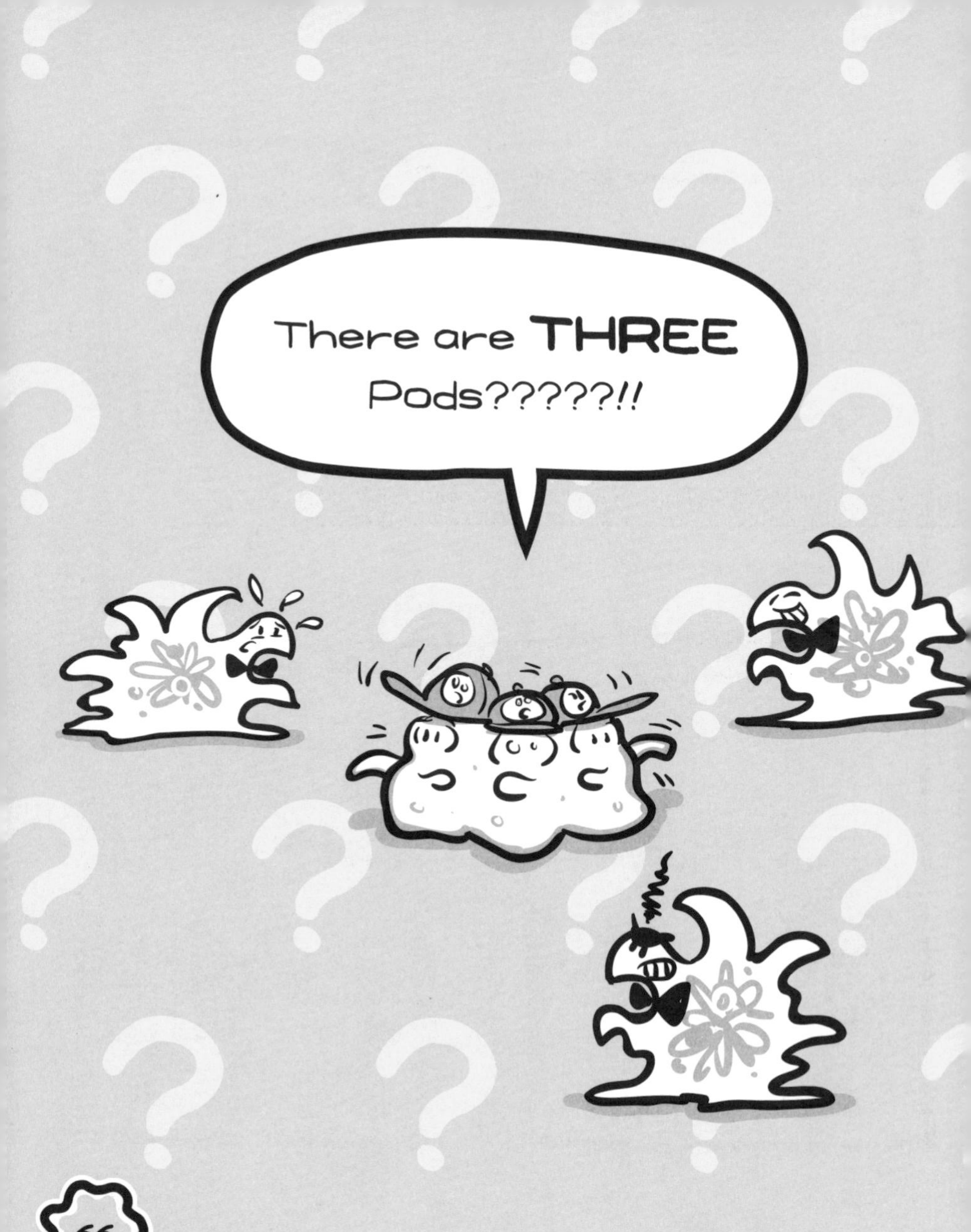
There are THREE Pods??????!!

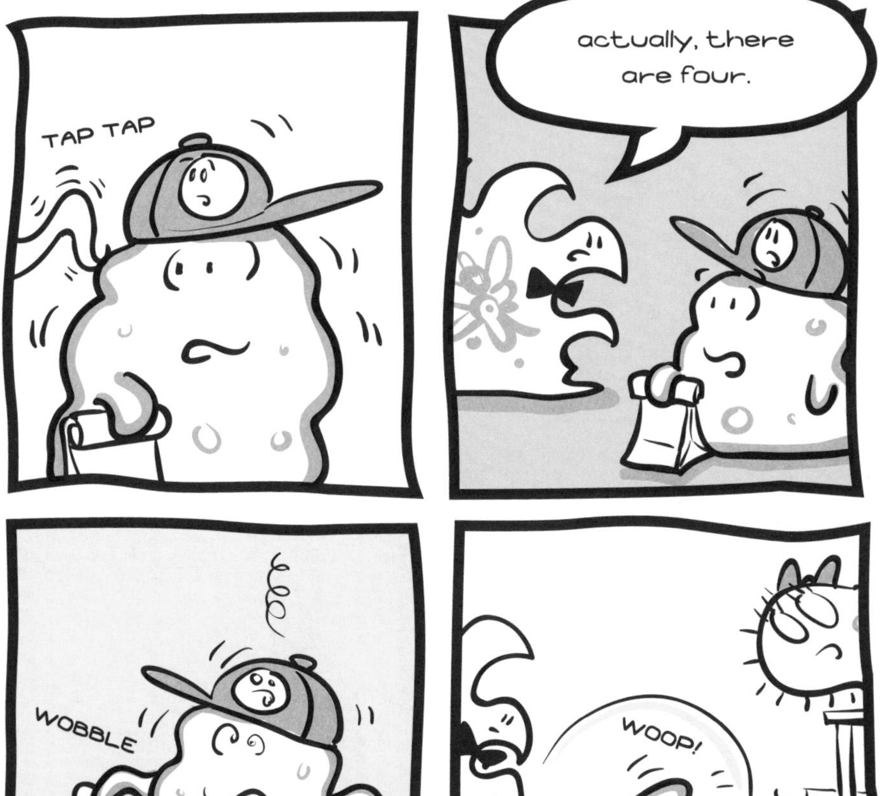
TAP TAP
actually, there are four.
WOBBLE
WOOP!
CRASH!

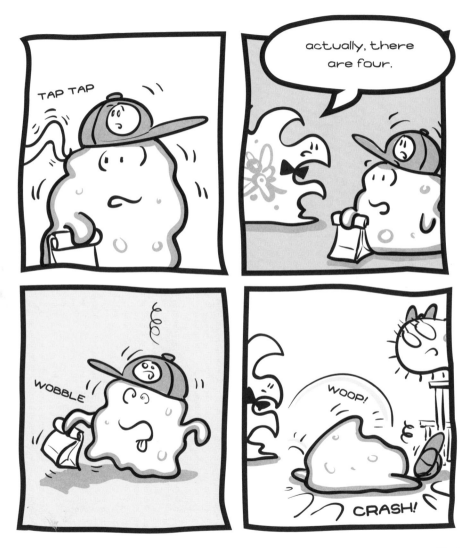

i guess he
won't be eating
his lunch.

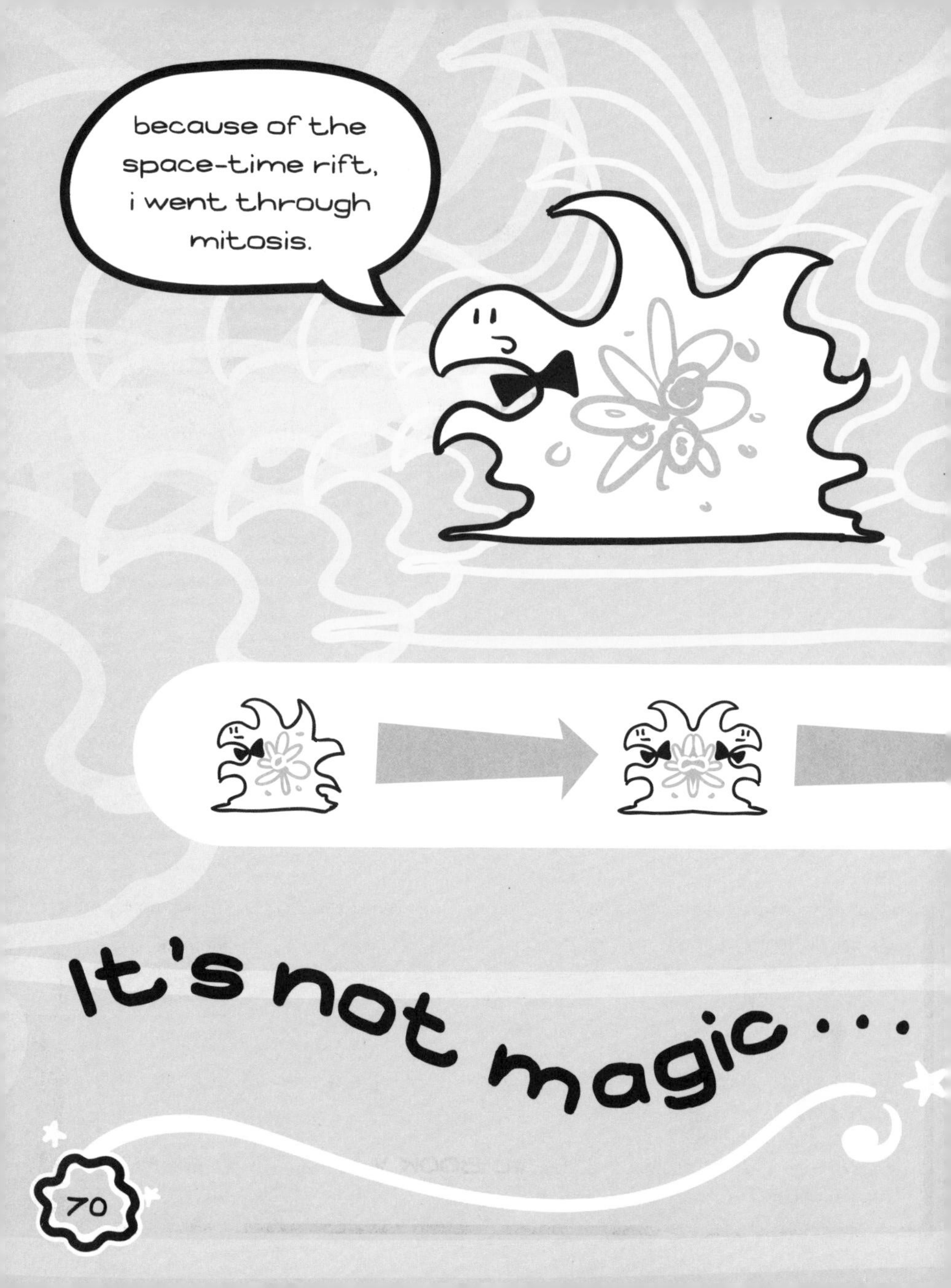
because of the space-time rift, i went through mitosis.
It's not magic...

it's...
MITOSIS!

*TRUE SCIENCE FACT: MITOSIS IS A REAL PROCESS! AMOEBAS AND MANY OTHER SINGLE-CELLED CREATURES SPLIT THEMSELVES IN TWO IN ORDER TO REPRODUCE!

**THEY USUALLY DON'T NEED A SPACE-TIME RIFT, THOUGH.

***WHAT GOOD IS A COMIC BOOK WITHOUT A SPACE-TIME RIFT?

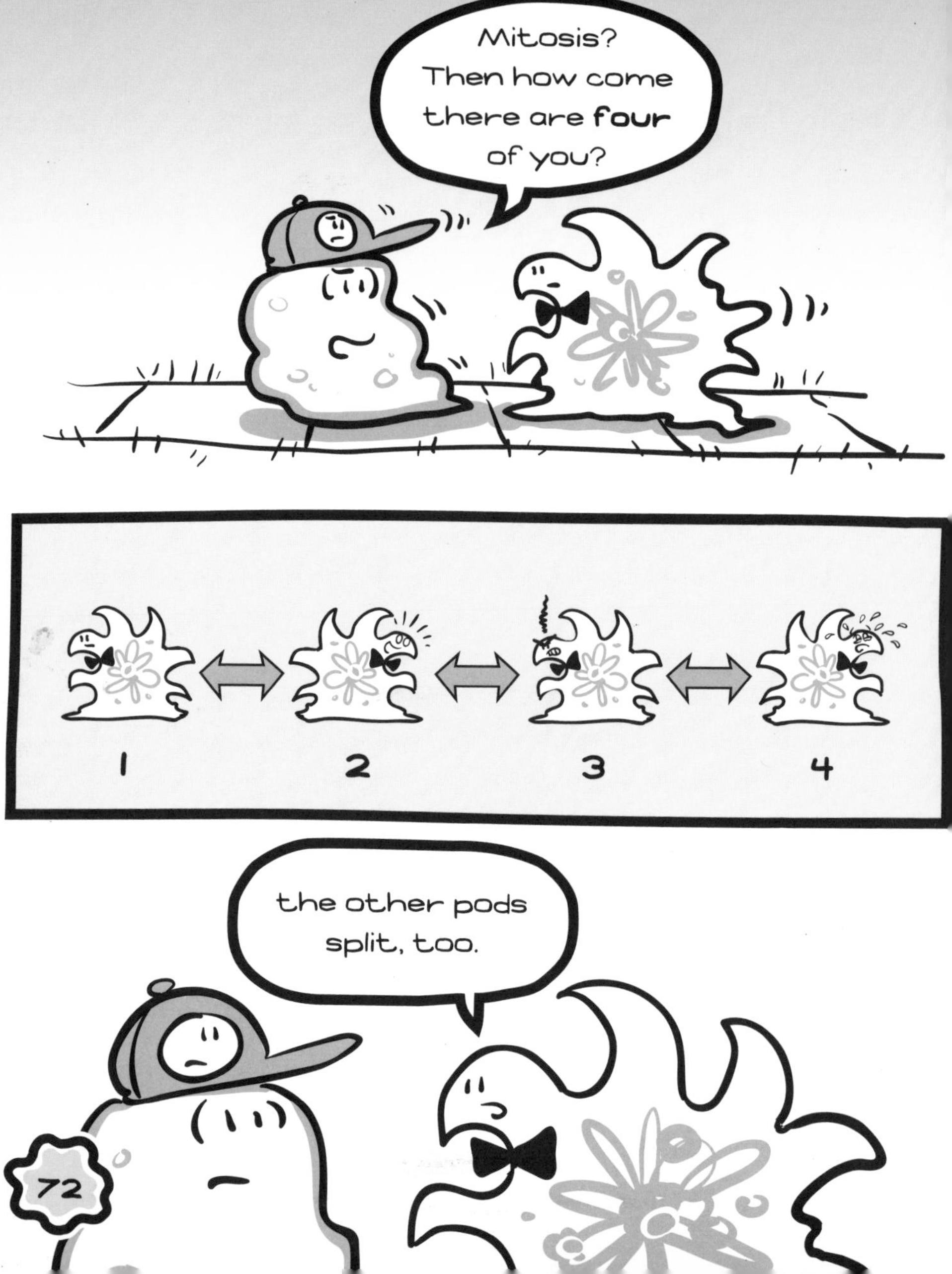
Mitosis? Then how come there are **four** of you?
1
2
3
4
the other pods split, too.

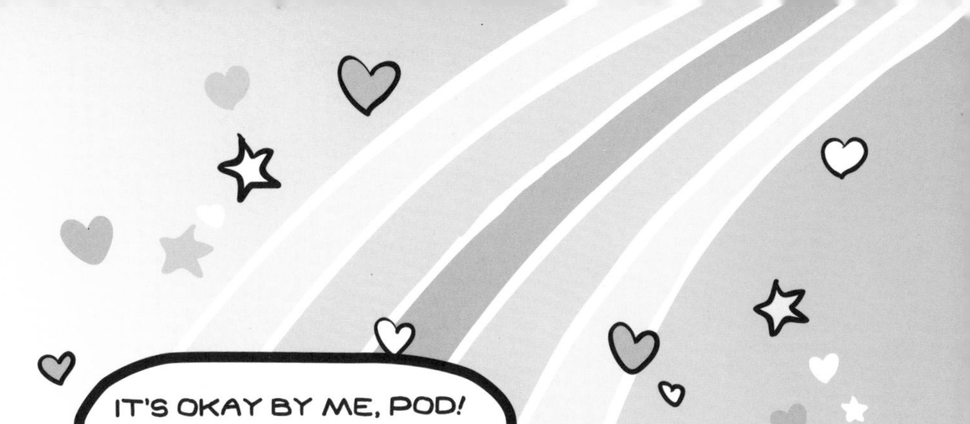
IT'S OKAY BY ME, POD! THERE'S JUST MORE OF YOU TO LOVE!

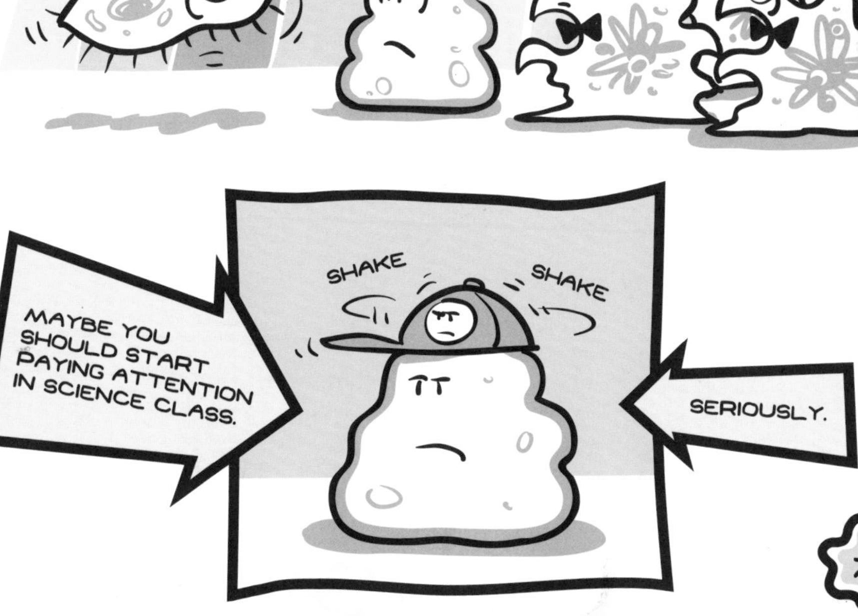
SHAKE
SHAKE
MAYBE YOU SHOULD START PAYING ATTENTION IN SCIENCE CLASS.
SERIOUSLY.

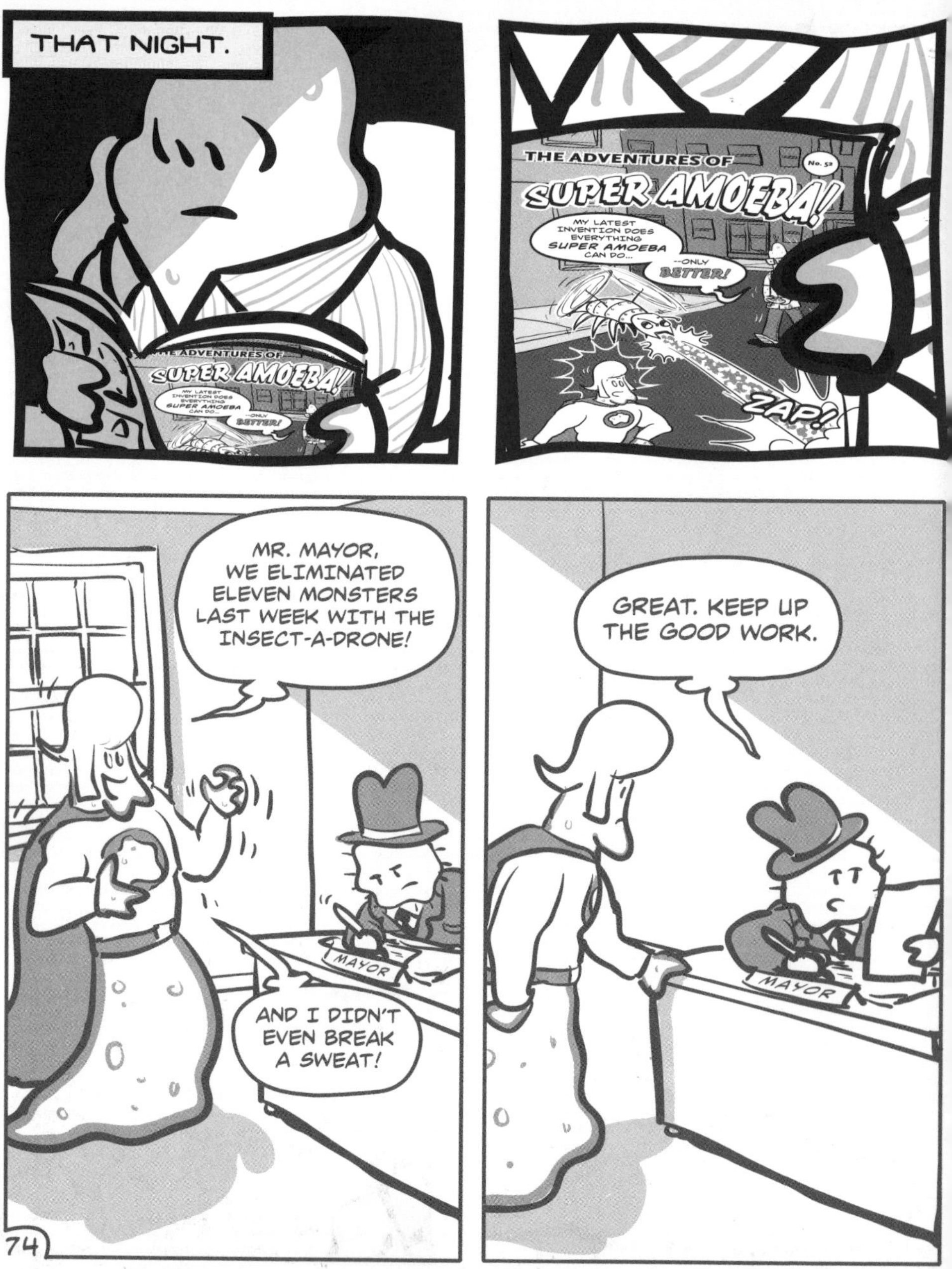
THAT NIGHT.
THE ADVENTURES OF
SUPER AMOEBA!
MY LATEST INVENTION DOES EVERYTHING SUPER AMOEBA CAN DO...
--ONLY BETTER!
THE ADVENTURES OF
No. 52
SUPER AMOEBA!
MY LATEST INVENTION DOES EVERYTHING SUPER AMOEBA CAN DO...
--ONLY BETTER!
ZAP!
MR. MAYOR, WE ELIMINATED ELEVEN MONSTERS LAST WEEK WITH THE INSECT-A-DRONE!
AND I DIDN'T EVEN BREAK A SWEAT!
MAYOR
GREAT. KEEP UP THE GOOD WORK.
MAYOR

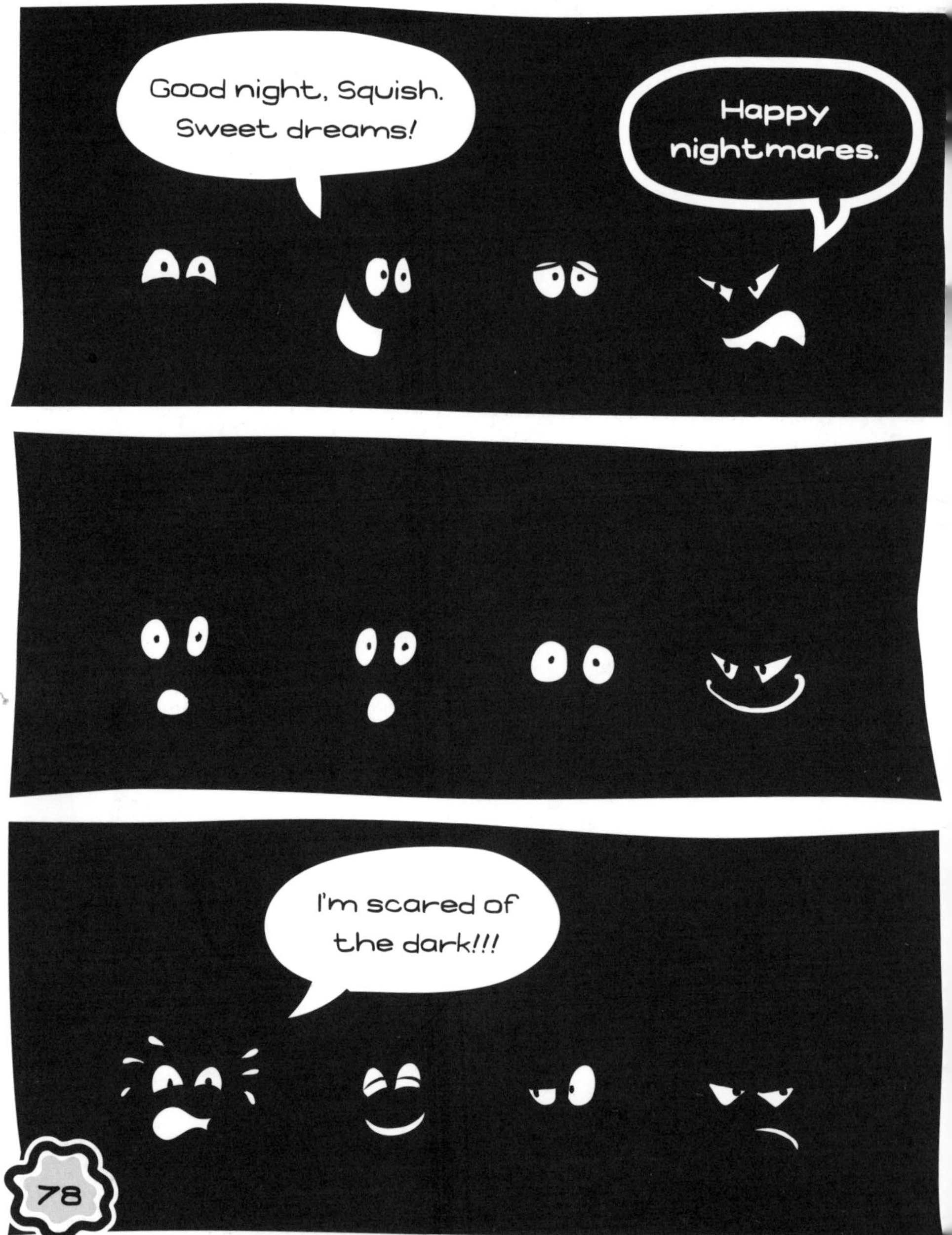
Good night, Squish. Sweet dreams!
Happy nightmares.
I'm scared of the dark!!!

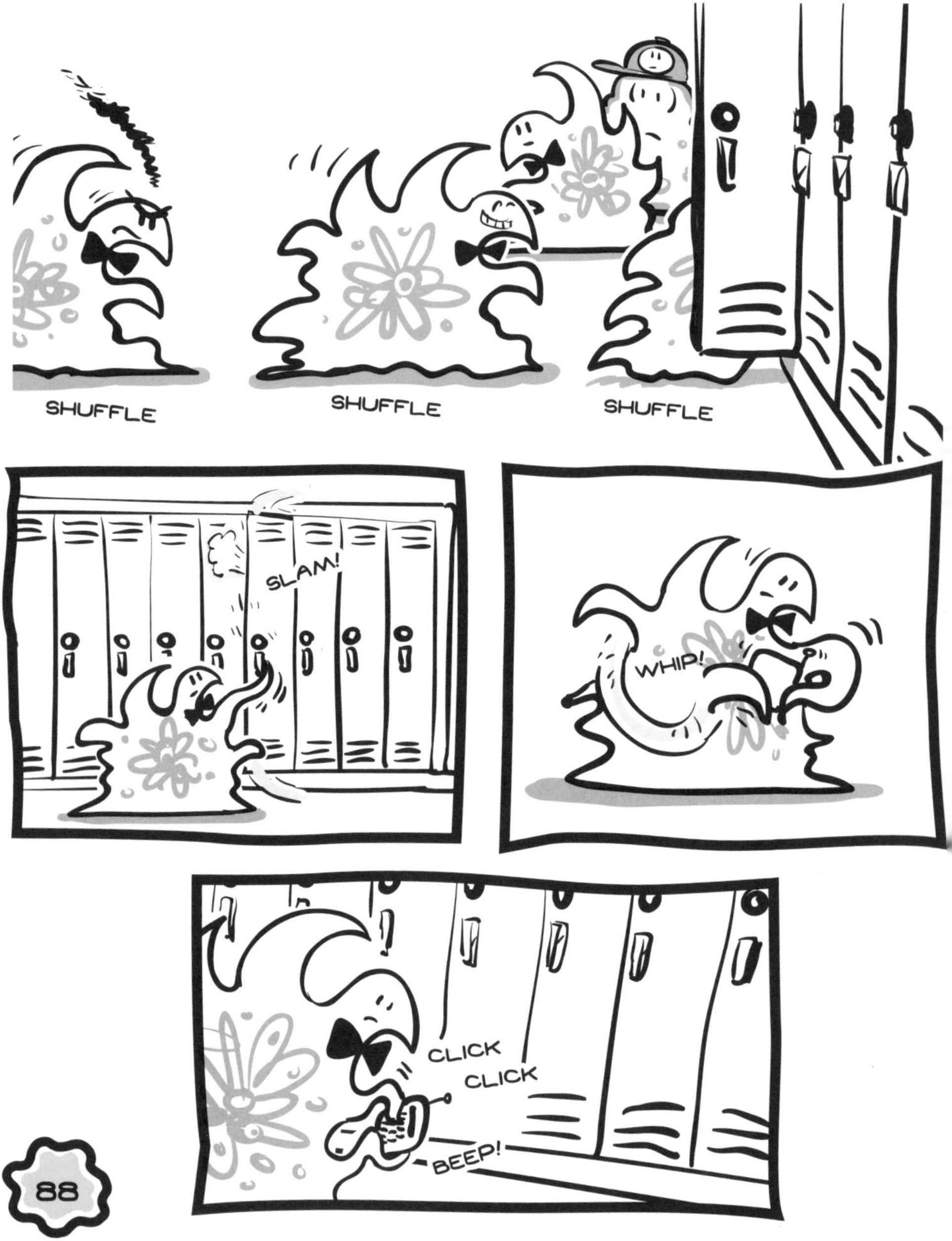
SHUFFLE
SHUFFLE
SHUFFLE
SLAM!
WHIP!
CLICK
CLICK
BEEP!

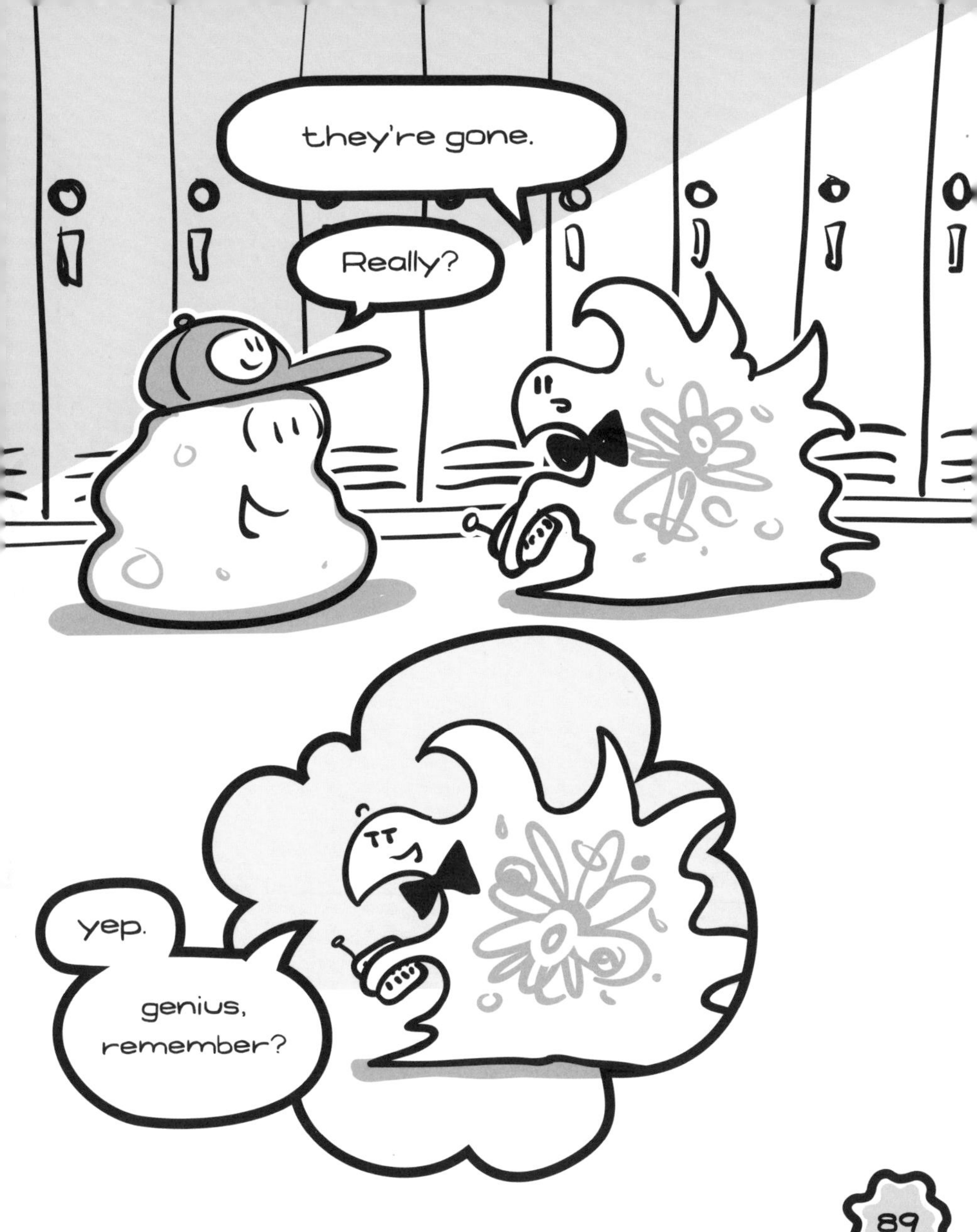

they're gone.
Really?
yep.
genius, remember?

FUN SCIENCE WITH POD!
hey, kids. want to learn how to tell a raw egg and a hard-boiled egg apart without breaking them?
it's easy. and fun.
get your supplies.
TWO EGGS
POT
WATER

IF YOU LIKE SQUISH, YOU'LL LOVE BABYMOUSE!

#1 BABYMOUSE: Queen of the World!
#2 BABYMOUSE: Our Hero
#3 BABYMOUSE: Beach Babe
#4 BABYMOUSE: Rock Star
#5 BABYMOUSE: Heartbreaker
#6 CAMP BABYMOUSE
#7 BABYMOUSE: Skater Girl
#8 BABYMOUSE: Puppy Love
#9 BABYMOUSE: Monster Mash
#10 BABYMOUSE: The Musical
#11 BABYMOUSE: Dragonslayer
#12 BABYMOUSE: Burns Rubber
#13 BABYMOUSE: Cupcake Tycoon
#14 BABYMOUSE: Mad Scientist
#15 A Very BABYMOUSE Christmas
#16 BABYMOUSE for President
#17 Extreme BABYMOUSE
#18 Happy Birthday, BABYMOUSE!
#19 BABYMOUSE: Bad Babysitter
#20 BABYMOUSE Goes for the Gold

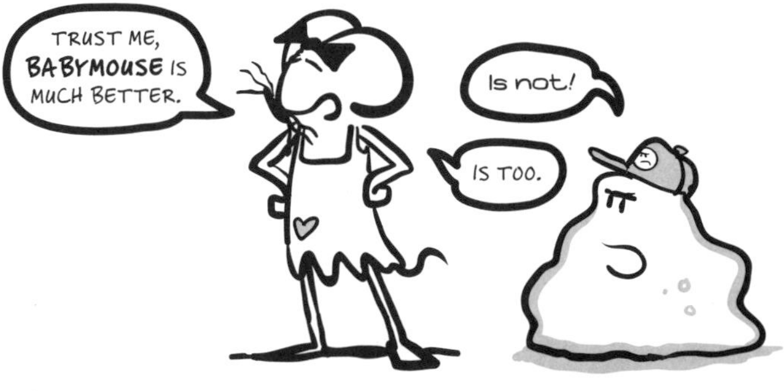
TRUST ME, BABYMOUSE IS MUCH BETTER.
Is not!
IS TOO.